# THE MEDICINE MAN

# THE MEDICINE MAN

*by*
Francisco Rojas González

*Translated by*
Robert S. Rudder and Gloria Arjona

Latin American Literary Review Press
Series: Discoveries
2000

The Latin American Literary Review Press publishes Latin American creative writing under the series title Discoveries, and critical works under the series title Explorations.

Library of Congress Cataloging-in-Publication Data

Rojas Gonález, Francisco, 1903-1951.
   [Diosero. English]
   The medicine man / by Francisco Rojas González; translated by Robert S. Rudder and Gloria Arjona.
     p.cm.
   ISBN 1-891270-07-9 (pbk.)
     1. Indians of Mexico--Fiction. I. Rudder, Robert S. II. Chacón de Arjona, Gloria. III.
   Title

   PQ7297.R74 D513 2000
   863--dc21                            99-058259

Cover design by David Wallace.

Latin American Literary Review Press
121 Edgewood Avenue
Pittsburgh, PA 15218

**NATIONAL
ENDOWMENT
FOR THE ARTS**

## *Acknowledgments*

This project is supported in part
by grants from the
National Endowment for the Arts in Washington, D.C.,
a federal agency,
and the
Commonwealth of Pennsylvania
Council on the Arts.

This English translation of *The Medicine Man*
is dedicated to the memory of our mothers,
Esther Baca Escudero de Chacón
and Nora Geneva Sween Rudder,
both women of medicine.

R.S.R.
G.A.

# CONTENTS

# The Medicine Man ⬎

Seated before me, Kai-Lan, lord of the Caribe Indian huts of Puná, assumes a graceful, ape-like posture and offers me a friendly smile; his stubby, restless hands fiddle with a reed. We are under the roof of his palm leaf hut, erected in a clearing in the jungle, a clearing that is a barren island, lost in an ocean of vegetation that threatens to overflow in rustling, black waves. As Kai-Lan listens, his eyes remain steady on my face; he appears to read my expression better than he understands my words. At times, when my meaning seems to penetrate the mind or heart of the Indian, he laughs, he laughs loudly... But at other times, when my narration turns serious, the Lacandón becomes somber and is apparently interested in the conversation, participating in it with a few monosyllables or with some simple phrase or other that he utters with difficulty.

Kai-Lan's three women are near us, his three *kikas*. Jacinta, nearly a child herself, and already the mother of an Indian baby—a little girl with round face and fat cheeks, still nursing; Jova, a reserved old woman, ugly and distant; and Nachak'in, a woman in full bloom: her profile arrogant, like a stone mask from Chichén-Itzá, her eyes sensuous and coquettish, her body shapely, desirable in spite of her short stature and gestures so loose that they become licentious along-side the dullness of the other two.

Kneeling next to the *metate*, the stone for grinding corn, Jova slaps out large circles of corn-dough; Jacinta, holding her daughter with her left arm, turns a pheasant, cut open from top to bottom, over the hot coals of a brazier, as it gives off an agreeable smell. Nachak'in, standing, dressed in her long, loose woolen shirt, looks boldly at her bustling companions.

"And that one," I asked Kai-Lan, pointing to Nachak'in, "why isn't she working?"

The Lacandón smiles, he is silent for a few seconds; in this way he gives the impression that he's searching for the proper words to use in his reply:

"She does not work during the day," he says finally, "at night she does… It is her turn to climb into Kai-Lan's hammock."

The beautiful *kika*, as though she understood the words that her husband has spoken to me in Spanish, lowers her eyes in response to my curious gaze, and peals back her lips in a terribly picaresque smile. From her short, robust neck hangs a necklace of alligator teeth.

Outside the hut, the jungle, the stage where the drama of the Lacandones unfolds. Opposite the house of Kai-Lan rises the temple of which he is High Priest and at the same time acolyte and parishio-ner. The temple is a hut, roofed with palm-leaves; it has only one wall, facing west; inside, rustic looking benches, and upon them incensories or braziers made of crude clay, the deities that control the passions, that temper the natural phenomena which unleash themselves in the jungle with diabolical fury, tamers of beasts, sanctuary against serpents and other reptiles, and shelter from wicked men who live beyond the forests.

Next to the temple, the patch of corn, carefully cultivated; between the sides of the furrows dug with a hoe, vigorous plants rise from the ground more than a foot high; a blanket of thorny sticks protects the field from the incursion of wild boars and tapirs, and down below, among vines and roots, the river Jataté. The weather is warm and humid.

The voice of the jungle, with its unchanging tone and its stubborn will—like the sea—this tumult that has enervating effects on anyone who hears it for the first time, and that eventually becomes a pleasant flurry during the day and a soft lullaby at night, this voice borne from the beaks of birds, the throats of beasts, from brittle branches, from the song of the leaves of silk-cotton trees, from the foliage and the murderous strangler-fig that stretches its tentacles tightly around the corpulent trunks of the mahogany tree, of the *sapodilla*, as it climbs, to extract their last drop of sap for itself, from the intermittent whistling of the *nauyaca*-snake that lives in the bark of the *chacalté*, and from the wailing cry of the *sarahuato*, a grotesque and cynical little monkey that romps about with its incessant screeching, hanging from vines or clambering unbelievably in the highest bowers... In such a din one can scarcely hear a word of the Lacandón who is lord of the jungle and at the same time the weakest and most dispossessed of all that gives life to this world of frond and light, noise and silence.

In the hut of Kai-Lan, chief of Puná, I await the dish that his exquisite hospitality has offered to me, so that after this treat I may go on my way, through breaches and quagmires into the green vastness and the marsh, toward the huts of Pancho Viejo, that silent, solitary, languid, Lacandón gentleman whose hut, bereft of *kikas*, rises down the Jataté river, a few kilometers from the lands of my present host. I figure that I'll be there by nightfall.

As I'm finishing off the breast of pheasant, Kai-Lan shows signs of uneasiness. He turns toward the jungle, he crinkles up his nose like a carnivorous animal catching the scent of something; he gets to his feet, and slowly walks outside. I watch as he questions the clouds; then, from the ground, he picks up a small stick and holds it between his thumb and first-finger; through the arch formed by his fingers, the sun can be seen, nearly at its zenith.

Kai-Lan has turned around, and he tells me the result of his observation.

"You will not go far... Water is coming, much water."

I insist that I must reach the huts of Pancho Viejo that very evening, but Kai-Lan hammers on cordially.

"Look, water comes soon," and he shows me the stick through which he has observed the clouds.

"Pancho Viejo is expecting me."

Kai-Lan no longer speaks.

I have risen to my feet. I stroke the cheek of the tiny one who has fallen asleep in her mother's arms, and as I prepare to leave, enormous drops of water stop me; the storm has unleashed itself. Kai-Lan smiles as he sees his prediction carried out: "Water... much water."

Immediately, beneath a ceiling the color of steel that has thrust itself between the jungle and the sun, a thunderbolt roars; the storm descends upon the profusion of tree branches scraping against the crusts of clouds. The voice of the jungle becomes hushed so that the clamor of the downpour of rain may be heard. The hut shudders violently; Kai-Lan sits down again, next to me; I am caught up by the spectacle that I'm witnessing for the first time.

The water rises visibly. Jacinta has left her child lying on Kai-Lan's hammock, and followed by Jova, with innocent lewdness they lift their shirts above the waist and begin to set up a dike inside the hut to stop the water from running in. Nachak'in, the *kika* this time, passes the time squatting in a corner of the hut. Kai-Lan, with chin in his hands, watches as the storm increases in intensity and rumbling.

"What do you want at Pancho Viejo's?" he suddenly asks me.

Without much desire to draw out the conversation, I answer somewhat sharply:

"He's going to tell me things about the life of you Caribe Indians."

"And what do you care? There is no reason to meddle in the lives of neighbors!" says the Lacandón without trying to wound me.

I do not reply.

Jacinta has taken her little daughter in her arms and holds her close to her breast; now there are shadows of worry on the young woman's face. Stoically, Jova begins cutting apart an enormous *sarahuato*. The animal's pelt, pierced by one of Kai-Lan's arrows, comes falling off the reddish flesh until a naked body is left, very similar in volume and close in form to that of the chubby-cheeked little Indian girl crying in Jacinta's arms.

Kai-Lan has asked me for a cigarette and from it he puffs great clouds of smoke that, as soon as they leave his mouth, are swept away by the storm.

In the meantime the sky has never ceased to spill its water-pouch out over the jungle. The clouds become a blur with the tops of the *chacalté* and the *sapota*-tree. A bolt of lightning has split apart the trunk of a centenary silk-cotton tree like a common piece of bamboo. The crash stuns us, and for a few seconds the livid light leaves us blinded.

In the hut no one speaks. The superstitious fear of the Indians is less than my fright as a civilized man.

"Water, much water…" Kai-Lan finally remarks.

Suddenly a drawn-out noise puts the finishing touch on our uneasiness. It is rotund like the sound of rocks wrenching apart. It is absolute, like the thunder of one hundred mahogany tree-trunks shattering in unison.

Kai-Lan stands up, he peers outside through the thick curtain unfurled by the storm. He speaks to the women in Lacandón, and they look out to the place where the man is pointing. I do the same.

"The river, it is the river," Kai-Lan says to me in Spanish.

In fact, the Jataté has become swollen; its waters hurl along tree-trunks, branches, stones as though they were straw.

The Lacandón speaks once more to his wives; they listen without a word. Jova goes to the rear of the hut and mixes together a pile of dry earth with her hands, while Kai-Lan, carrying a large gourd, walks out into the storm and immediately returns, his hair, soaking-wet, dangling down past his shoulders. The shirt sticks to his body, making him appear ridiculous… Now, over the earth he pours the water from the gourd that he has brought inside. The women watch him, filled with devotion. Kai-Lan repeats the process again and again. The water and earth have become clay that the small man kneads. When he has come to the point where the clay is doughy and malleable, he sets out once again into the center of the storm. We watch him go into the temple and break apart the brazier-deities with mystical fury. As soon as he has finished with the last one, he comes back to the hut.

"The gods are old… they are useless now," he tells me. "I will make another one, strong and brave, who will put an end to the water."

… And, stretched out before the mound of clay, Kai-Lan, with unexpected mastery, begins to mold a new incensory, a magnificent and powerful god, capable of exorcising the clouds that now unleash themselves upon the huts and the river.

Discreetly, the *kikas* have turned their backs to the man. They speak to one another in hushed tones. Suddenly Nachak'in risks a glance that Kai-Lan catches sight of. The small man has risen to his feet, he shouts harshly, he claps his hands in the air, overcome with rage. Nachak'in, facing the wall again, her head down, humbly endures the reprimand... Convulsed with anger, Kai-Lan has torn apart the work that is nearly finished. God has succumbed once more to the hands of man.

After the Lacandón has made certain that the impure eye of the females will not defile the divine work, he tries to construct it once again.

...And there it is, a beautiful incensory of zoomorphic appearance. A potbellied bird, its back sunken in the shape of a saucepan, the tiny figure holds itself erect on three feet that end in cleft hoofs like those of a boar. Two chips of flint gleam from deep within their cavities. Kai-Lan shows that he is well satisfied with his work. He looks it up and down. He touches it again, he smooths its surface... He studies it at a distance, from every angle. And finally he conceals it under the flounce of his tunic, and goes out with it, into the storm, toward the temple... Now he is there. I see him through the dim crystal of the squall. He enthrones the resplendent god, still fresh, upon the stand. On its back he throws grains of *copal* and some live coals that he picks up with two sticks from the perpetual flame burning in the center of the room. Kai-Lan remains standing, motionless, hieratic, his arms folded, his head held high.

Meanwhile, Jova stirs the fire and it crackles, the flames slightly illuminating the hut where darkness has begun to take form. The wind continues amid the groans of trees being torn apart and the thunder of torrents. The Jataté has become arrogant, its waters are rising to an alarming height... Now they threaten to overflow. Already they are lapping at the banks that protect the cornfield. Kai-Lan has seen the danger. Beneath the roof of the temple he uneasily observes the threatening attitude of the river. He turns toward the brazier, he fills it again with resin, and he waits. But the storm does not yield. The heavy clouds sway in the summits and their shadows fall over the Caribe huts. Night rushes in... I see the silhouette of

Kai-Lan as he goes to the altar. He takes the god in his hands. He destroys it and then, in a rage, hurls the fragments of clay into the pools of water that have formed in front of his hut... Useless god, unworthy god, stupid god...!

But Kai-Lan has left the temple and he is going to the cornfield. It is a struggle to move through the waters. Now he gets down on all fours next to the river. He looks like a tapir wallowing in the mire. He drags over large tree-trunks and branches, rocks and foliage. With all of it, he shores up the planted field. His work is agonizing and ineffectual. As I start out to help him, he returns to the hut, convinced that his efforts are useless. Then, violently, he harangues the women, and they turn their faces once again toward the wall of palm-leaves. The child sleeps peacefully on the hammock, her fat, little body lying among filthy, wet rags.

Kai-Lan sets himself to the task once more.

And now, before us, we have the new god that has sprung forth from his magical hands. This one is more massive than the previous one, but less beautiful. The Lacandón raises it to the level of his eyes and contemplates it for a few seconds. He seems very proud of his creation. Behind him we hear the wailing of the child who has perhaps been awakened by the sting of an insect. When Kai-Lan turns he finds the little one staring at the incensory. The Lacandón has a look of impatience that, with the baby's laughter, soon turns to a benevolent smile. He throws the incensory, now blemished by the eyes of a female, onto the floor and begins to smash it with his bare feet. When he has finally destroyed it, he cries out. Not daring to raise her head, Jacinta picks up her daughter and carries her in her arms over to the wall. Through the sleeve of her shirt she pulls out an enormous, dark teat that the child grasps. Jacinta, like the other *kikas*, has turned her face away from Kai-Lan who does not lose faith. Now he begins again.

The Indian puts so much energy into his work that he forgets about me, and I freely watch the steps in the manufacture of the god as they take place... Kai-Lan's small hands take pieces of clay, they nervously roll around balls, they mold cylinders or smooth out flat shapes; they dance over the incipient form, intent, agile, lively. Jova and Jacinta, the latter rocking the child in her arms, remain standing, their backs to us. Nachak'in, melancholy perhaps because of the

frustration of her seduction, is sitting, cross-legged, facing the wall.
Her head slumps, she is fast asleep. In the center of the hut the fire
crackles. It is nighttime.

This time the making of the god has been more laborious. One
could say that, confronted by the failures, the maker puts all his art,
all his mastery to the task. He sculpts a fabulous quadruped: snout
of a *nauyaca*-snake, body of a tapir and the enormous, graceful tail
of a *quetzal*-bird. Now, silently, he looks at the fruit of his efforts.
There it is, a magnificent beast, strong, dark, brutal... The Lacandón
has risen to his feet; the incensory rests on the floor. Kai-Lan takes a
few steps backward to look at it from a distance. He has noticed
some imperfection that he hastens to correct with his fingers moistened with saliva... Finally, he is completely satisfied. He lifts the
incensory in his arms, and when he is certain that it has not been
profaned by the look of females, he smiles and prepares to take it to
his altars. He brushes against my legs as he goes past; I am certain
that at this instant he does not notice my presence at all.

The shadows of the rain-soaked night do not allow me to see
the handiwork of Kai-Lan in his function as High Priest. My eyes
can barely make out the tiny, intermittent light that burns on the
back of the newly-sculpted deity, and the anguished flickering of the
fire, fed perpetually with wet wood.

In the meantime, Jova has built a marvelous structure of sticks
next to the hearth. From it the *sarahuato* hangs, to be cooked over
the embers. The appearance of the quadruped is awful. Its head,
slumped over its chest seems to be grimacing; its twisted limbs remind me of figures of martyrs, of male martyrs being subjected to
torture because of their saintliness or... their heresy. The grains of
salt that spatter the flesh burst with a small, enervating crackle, while
fat drips down to leave the little, anthropomorphic body black and
dried-out.

Jacinta, kneeling before a potbellied piece of earthenware, takes
out the corn and places it on the grinding stone. The child is sleeping on a mat spread out within the mother's reach.

Nachak'in, who is seeing her night of love pass by fruitlessly,
has thrown herself upon the hammock where she frets anxiously.
Her legs, shapely and small, hang down and swing back and forth
restlessly.

Suddenly we hear shouts coming from the cornfield. It is Kai-Lan. Jacinta and Jova respond immediately to the call; the two *kikas* go out into the storm, to where their husband is summoning them. Nachak'in barely sits up to watch them go. She yawns, she folds her arms over the head of the hammock and stretches her body like a small beast in heat.

I look out toward the field. Kai-Lan under a lush silk-cotton tree holds up a stick of candlewood whose flame, surprisingly, challenges the violent wind. The women struggle in the midst of the mud in furious battle against the water that has already risen above the small ledge that had held it back. Now the first stalks of corn are under water. I run to help the women. Immediately I find myself sunk to the waist in mud and engaged in the Lacandones' fight. While Jacinta and I bring up stones and mud, Jova builds a barrier that, more swiftly than it can be raised, is torn away by the current. Kai-Lan cries out stinging words in Lacandón; they redouble their efforts. The man comes and goes under the enormous umbrella of the silk-cotton trees; the torch, held aloft, sends out its weak light to us. A moment arrives when Kai-Lan's agitation is irrepressible. He leaves the stick of candlewood propped up between two stones and goes toward the temple-hut. He enters and leaves us engaged in our useless efforts... Jacinta has slipped and fallen. The water drags her a distance. Jova is able to grab her by the hair and with my help we pull her out of danger. An enormous tree trunk floating in the water completely sweeps away our work... The flood overflows now into rivulets that make pools of water at the feet of the *maize*-plants. Nothing can be done. And yet, the women keep up their earnest fight. When I am at the point of leaving, absolutely exhausted, I notice that the storm is over... It has gone just as it came, without spectacular circumstances, suddenly, just the way everything in the jungle appears or leaves: the predators, lightning, the wind, vegetation, death...

Kai-Lan emerges from the temple, he cries out jubilantly. Nachak'in peers out from the hut and celebrates her husband's happiness with laughter. We go back to the hut.

Nachak'in sees how the monkey's body is becoming scorched, is turning to char, and does nothing to stop it. A black, fetid cloud makes the air unbreathable. The child sobs, exhausted from its wailing.

The women laugh when they see how ridiculous I look: we are smeared with mud from head to foot.

I try to clean the mud from my boots. Kai-Lan offers me a gourd full of *balché*, the fermented drink that is a ritual for great occasions. I take one drink, then another and another... When I bend my elbow for the third time I notice that dawn is breaking.

Kai-Lan is at my side, he is looking at me amiably. Nachak'in comes up and tries to wrap her arm around the small man's neck, lewdly and provocatively. He pushes her back delicately and at the same time says to me:

"Not Nachak'in now, because today is tomorrow."

Then, softly, he calls to Jova. The old woman comes to the man submissively. He puts his arm around her waist and leaves it there.

"Today Jova will not work... She will at night, because it is her turn to climb into Kai-Lan's hammock."

Then he says a few brief, terse words to Nachak'in who has distanced herself slightly from the group. The beautiful, imperious woman, now docile and humble, goes to the hearth to take the place that Jova, whose turn it is to be *kika,* has left.

I make ready to go. I give some red combs and a mirror to the women. They show their gratitude with wide, white smiles.

Kai-Lan presents me with a ham of monkey that escaped the scorching. I repay him with a handful of cigarettes.

I start out in the direction of the huts of the gentleman, Pancho Viejo. Kai-Lan accompanies me to the rough ground. When we pass by the temple, the Lacandón stops and, pointing to the altar, he remarks:

"There is no one, in all the jungle, like Kai-Lan for making gods... It turned out well, did it not? It killed the storm... Look, in the struggle it lost its beautiful tail of the *quetzal*-bird and left it in the sky."

In fact, caught on the bower of a tree, a rainbow appears, resplendent...

# The Tona ⁀

Crisanta was walking down the path that snaked through the boulders of the hillock. This lay between the tiny village and the rough river that was fed by rapid streams forcing their way through rockrose and wild grasses, hurling themselves ahead and dragging along chunks of bark as they snatched them from oak trees on the hill. Spreading out into the valley, Tapijulapa, the village of sheep-herding Indians. The small towers of the chapel, damp with fervors, grimy from passing years, pierced the cloud that lay imprisoned in the arms of the iron cross.

Crisanta, a young Indian woman, nearly a child herself, walked down the path; the late-afternoon air sent shivers through her body, bent under the weight of a bundle of firewood; her head hanging down, and above her forehead, a clump of hair soaking with sweat. Her feet—now claws; now hoofs—slipped on flat stones, sank into lichens, or settled like the limbs of a heavy-footed animal onto the level ground of the little path… The woman's thighs, dark and solid, peaked at torn places in the cotton skirt that she lifted in front of her, all the way over her knees, because her belly was straining with pregnancy… Walking became more painful with every step; at moments the girl stopped to catch her breath; but then, without lifting her head, she moved forward again with all the vehemence of a beast attacking the specter of air.

But a moment came when her legs refused to go any further, they faltered. Crisanta lifted her head for the first time, and her eyes wandered over the land beyond. A veil of anguish fell over the small Zoque woman's face; her lips trembled and her nostrils pulsed as though picking up a scent. With faltering steps, the Indian woman sought out the river's edge, seemingly carried along by instinct more than guided by thought. The river was close at hand, not more than twenty steps from the footpath. When she came to its edge, she loosened the *mecapal*, the porter's strap tied around her forehead, and with a great effort deposited the bundle of wood on the ground; then, as all Zoque women do, all of them...

grandmother,

mother,

sister,

friend,

enemy,

...she pulled her torn skirt above her waist and squatted down, legs open, her hands tightly gripping rough, bruised knees. She made an effort to bear the stabbing pain. She breathed deeply, irregularly, as if all human emotion had taken root in her throat. Then she made her hands, those hard hands, cracked and wrinkled from hard labor, into instruments of relief, stroking her large abdomen that was now convulsed and cramping. Tears, springing from the overflowing sclera, slid from her eyes. But every effort was in vain. She stretched her fingers, the only means of relief, down to the hot, swollen inner surface of her thighs, and then took them away because they were ineffectual... Then she thrust them violently into the ground, holding them there, straining in fury and desperation... Suddenly thirst became one more torture... and there she went, dragging her body along like a coyote, until she reached the river; stretched out on the sand, she attempted to drink, but nausea welled up each time she tried to swallo...w; then she moaned in desperation, rolling convulsively in the sand. And this was how her husband, Simón, found her.

When the young man reached his Crisanta, she received him with harsh words in the Zoque tongue; but Simón had become deaf.

He lifted her gently in his arms and led her back to their dwelling, a straw thatched hut, embedded in the side of the hill. The slight man deposited the tremulous load of two lives onto the palm-mat and went out in search of Altagracia, the old midwife who was dying of hunger in this village where women gave birth by themselves, all alone, on the bank of the river, with no assistance other than their own hands, their exertions and their moans.

Altagracia came to the hut, Simón following behind. The old woman lit a handful of pitch-pine and left it burning over a pot; then, with complicated gestures and mysterious actions, she quickly knelt on the hardened ground and prayed the Creed in reverse, beginning with "Amen," and ending with "…the Father, in God, I believe." According to her, it was a first-rate way to get a person out of the worst mess imaginable. Then she went on, touching the swollen belly in various places.

"Don't worry, Simón; we'll have her fixed up right away. This always happens with the first ones… Hmm, I don't know how many times I've had to battle them…!" she said.

"May God give his help," answered the boy as he threw a resinous chip of wood on the fire.

"Did your pains start long ago, child?"

In reply, Crisanta could give only a murmur.

"Let's see, girl," continued Altagracia; "bend your knees… That's it, keep them loose. Breathe deep, push, push hard whenever the pain comes… Harder, harder… Scream, child…!"

Crisanta did everything she was told to and more; her legs were like rags; she screamed until she was hoarse, she bit her fists till they were bloody.

"Come on, help me, girl," begged the old woman, roughly moving her hands over the belly that was relaxed, but stubborn in holding onto its load…

And the able fingers with crooked, black nails worked with all their skill, all their experience, all their dexterity, massaging, beginning with the round breasts and ending at the massive, hairless pelvis.

Simón, meanwhile, sat crouched in a corner of the hut; between his legs was a piece of wood that would eventually become the handle of a spade. The scraping noise of the file that he used to sharpen one end of the handle diverted the boy's attention from his unsteadiness, took away a little of his anxiety.

"Come on, little mother, scream as loud as you can... Push, give it all you got... Swear at me, call me names; but hurry it up... Give birth, you lazy thing. Give birth to a male or a female, but do it now... Christ of Esquipulas!"

The young woman made no effort now; pain had won out.

Now Simón was trying to pound the handle into the eye of the spade; hoarse noises came from his partly opened mouth.

Altagracia, sweaty and disheveled, her stiff hands open like a fan, turned toward the boy who had finally gotten the handle into the collar of the spade. The work had distanced his thoughts slightly from the place where the drama was playing out.

"It's no good at all, Simón; he's coming out rear end first," shouted the old woman as she wiped her forehead with the back of her right hand.

And Simón, as though waking from a dream, as if the intemperate words had taken him from some luminous, pleasant place:

"Rear end first? All right... an' now what?"

The old woman did not answer; her eyes wandered over the roof of the hut.

"There," she said suddenly, "from there. Hang that strap over the main beam so we can make a swinging tether out of it. But hurry, get a move on," ordered Altagracia.

"No, not that," he moaned.

"Come on, let's give it one last try... Hang up the strap and help me tie the girl under the arms."

Without wasting words, Simón used the knotted joints to climb the thatched walls; he passed the strap over the horizontal beam that held up the roof.

"Pull hard... hard, put something into it. Huh, you don't even look like a man...! Pull, you devil."

Crisanta was suddenly a puppet, her feet kicking, twisting, as she hung by the strap.

Altagracia pushed on the girl's body... Now, more than a rag doll, she was a pendulum of tragedy, a nipple of delirium...

But Crisanta did nothing more for her, she had fallen into a convulsive faint.

"Run, Simón," said Altagracia, alarmed, "go to the store and buy a *peso's* worth of dry chile. We'll have to put it on the fire so the smoke will make her cough. She can't do it by herself anymore; we're losing her… While you do that, I'll carry on my struggle with the help of God and the Virgin Mary… I'm going to tighten my shawl around her waist and see if he'll come out that way… Run like your life depended on it!"

Simón was no longer listening to the words of the old woman; he was gone, racing to carry out her demands.

On the road he bumped into his friend, Trinidad Pérez, the *peon* who lived on the unfinished highway that passed near Tapijulapa.

"Wait up, man, how about saying hello, at least," shouted Trinidad Pérez.

"The woman's been in labor since before the sun went down, and she still hasn't been able to give birth," the other man exclaimed without stopping.

Trinidad Pérez caught up with Simón, and the two of them ran together.

"Doña Altagracia is helping her… We've fought, but she isn't getting any better."

"Do you want some advice, Simón?"

"Go ahead…"

"Go to the camp where the highway engineers are. There's a doctor there. He's a very good man. Call him."

"And what do I pay him with?"

"If you tell him how poor we are, he'll understand… Go on, forget about Altagracia."

Simón made up his mind, and instead of turning toward the store, he took the quickest shortcut to the encampment. The moon, high above, told him that midnight was near.

Simón, the Zoque Indian, had no need to speak at any length and so display his bad Spanish to the doctor, an amiable, jocose old man.

"Why do women take a notion to work their miracles at this time of night?" the doctor asked himself, and a yawn smothered his last words… But after shaking off his sleep, he added good-humoredly: "Why do some of us men take a notion to be doctors? I'm coming, boy, I'm coming right now; this was all I needed… Is the road to your village any good?"

"As good, just as smooth, as the palm of your hand…"

The doctor put some nickel-plated instruments into his little bag, along with a hypodermic syringe and a large package of cotton. He stuck on his old Panama hat, tossed down a good swig of liquor from the bottle, fixed the cyclist bands over the cuffs of his twill trousers, and got onto his bicycle as he listened to Simón saying:

"When you turn left, it's the little house that's backed up against the hill."

When Simón came to his hut he was greeted by a long, sharp wail that was lost in the cackling of hens and the growling of Mit-Chueg, the faithful, golden-haired dog.

Simón removed a large grass handkerchief from the crown of his hat, and wiped the sweat that ran down his forehead; then, taking a deep breath, he timidly pushed open the small door of the hut.

Covered with a faded *serape*, Crisanta lay quietly. Altagracia was now removing a large jug of hot water from the fire, and the doctor, sleeves rolled up, was taking the needle out of the hypodermic syringe.

"We made a little boy," Crisanta said weakly in the agglutinative Zoque tongue as soon as she saw her husband. Then her mouth was lit by the gleam of two rows of teeth like tiny kernels of corn.

"A boy?" Simón inquired proudly. "Just like I said…"

After taking Crisanta's chin in his rough fingers, clumsy at caressing, he went over to look at his son whom the doctor and Altagracia were preparing to bathe. The new father, rough as a rock, watched that piece of cinnamon struggle and shriek.

"He's nice-looking," he said. "With his big lips, he looks like her," and he jutted his chin toward Crisanta. Then, with hard, clumsy fingers, he attempted to caress the cheek of the newborn child.

"Thank you, dear doctor… You made me the happiest man in Tapijulapa."

And without another word, the Indian went over to the hearth made of three rocks in the center of the hut. A large quantity of ash had accumulated there. Simón grabbed fistsful of ash and put them into a sack.

The doctor watched him, intrigued. The boy, paying no attention to the curiosity that he was causing, slung the bag over his back and left the hut.

"What's that man doing?" inquired the doctor.

Then Altagracia struggled to speak in Spanish:

"Simón will spread the ashes around the house... When the sun comes up he will go out again. Whatever animal leaves its footprints painted on the ashes will be the child's *tona*. He will take the name of the bird or the animal that came first to greet him; coyote or badger, humming bird, hare or blackbird, whatever which..."

"*Tona*, you said?"

"Yes, *tona* will take care of him and be his friend forever, until he dies."

"Ah," said the doctor, smiling, "it's a question of finding a guardian spirit for the boy..."

"Yes," agreed the old woman, "that's the custom around here..."

"All right, good. In the meantime let's give him a bath so that the one who's going to be his *tona* will find him a nice, clean boy."

When Simón came back, his sack of ashes empty now, he found his son, wrapped in cloth and fresh-looking, on the mother's shoulder. Crisanta was sleeping sweetly and deeply... The doctor was preparing to leave.

"All right, Simón," said the doctor. "You're all set."

"I would like to give you something, sir, even if it's nothin' more than just a little handful o' salt..."

"Forget it, old boy, it's all right... I'll bring you some medicine soon, so the child will grow up healthy and handsome..."

"Doctor, sir," added Simón in a grateful way, "do me another favor, if you'll be good enough."

"Tell me, fellow."

"I would like your honor to be my *compadre*... For you to baptize my baby. Do you mind?"

"I'd be glad to, Simón. You let me know."

"Wednesday, please. That's the day the priest comes."

"I'll be here Wednesday... Good night, Simón... Good-bye, Altagracia, take care of the girl and the child..."

Simón went to the door of the hut with the doctor. From there he watched him go. The bicycle took the bumps and dips in the road gracefully, its Cyclopean eye opening the way in the darkness. A startled rabbit darted across its path.

On Wednesday morning the doctor arrived right on time.

The bell pealed for mass, the Zoques, dressed in clean clothes, waited in the atrium. The oboe played happy tunes. Fireworks were set off. Everyone who had gathered there, men and women, anxiously awaited the arrival of Simón and his baptismal suite.

Over there, by the hill, the group could be seen coming toward the Church. Crisanta, fresh and happy, carrying her son, followed by Altagracia, the godmother. Behind them, Simón and the doctor were chatting amiably…

"And what name are you going to give to my godson, Simón, my friend?"

"Well, as you'll see, dear Doctor… Damián, because that's what the Church calendar says… And Bicycle, because that's his *tona*; that's what the ashes told me…"

"So then, Damián Bicycle? That's a fine name, my friend…"

"*Áxcale*, that's so," the Zoque agreed decisively.

# THE BETROTHED ⌒

He was from Bachajón; from a family of pottery-makers. Since the time his hands were tiny, they had learned to shape a figure, to turn the clay so delicately that as they sculpted they really seemed to be caressing. He was an only-child, but a certain restlessness that sprang from his heart had begun pulling him from his parents; day after day, he was carried along by a sweet vertigo... For some time the murmur of the brook had swept him along in ecstasy, while his heart beat unsteadily. Even the aroma of honey bees around the Easter lily came to charm him, and the sighs hidden in his breast slipped out silently, hidden, the way uneasiness springs up when a person has done something terribly wrong... At times a mournful little tune rested on his lips and he hummed it softly, as though selfishly enjoying a tart but very pleasing dish.

"A skirt has turned that boy's head," his father remarked when he accidentally happened on the singing.

Overcome with shame, the boy did not sing again; but the father—Juan Lucas, a Tzeltal Indian from Bachajón—had come into possession of his son's secret.

She was from Bachajón too; small, plump, and soft. Day after day, when she went to the brook for water, she passed by Juan Lucas's doorway... There, a young man sat before a vessel of soft clay, a pitcher—round and broad—that his skilled, untiring hands never quite put the finishing touches on...

One morning, only God knows how, two glances met. There was no spark, no flame, no fire after that meeting that scarcely managed to make the robin's wings flutter, nestled among the branches of the elm tree that grew in the little plot of ground.

And yet, from that moment, she began to shorten her steps whenever she passed the potter's house, and covertly she dared a glance filled with urgent timidity.

For his part, he halted his work for a moment, he raised his eyes and they embraced the silhouette that followed the path until it became lost in the foliage growing alongside the river.

It was a splendid afternoon when the father—Juan Lucas, a Tzeltal Indian from Bachajón—put aside the wheel on which he had been working a piece of pottery... He followed the boy's gaze with his own until it came to the place where his son's eyes rested... When she, the object, the intended one, felt the penetrating eyes of the old man upon her, she stood, petrified, in the middle of the path. Her head fell onto her chest, and she hid the blush that burned her cheeks.

"Is she the one?" the old man drily asked his son.

"Yes," answered the boy, and he took up his labor again to hide his confusion.

The *Prencipal*, an old Indian, venerable in years and imposing in prestige, listened attentively to Juan Lucas's request:

"The young man, same as an old one, needs female companionship: for the first it's a sweet-smelling flower, and for the other it's a help... My son has already laid his eyes on one."

"Let's carry out God's law and give pleasure to the boy the way you and I had it, Juan Lucas, in our day... You tell me what to do!"

"I want you to ask for the girl, for my son."

"That's my duty as *Prencipal*... Go on: I'll follow you, Juan Lucas."

Before the house of the chosen woman, Juan Lucas, carrying a pound of chocolate, several bunches of cigarettes, a load of firewood and another of pitch pine, stood beside the *Prencipal* of Bachajón, waiting for those who lived in the hut to answer the knock at their door.

Soon, native formality impregnates the entire atmosphere.

"Hail, Holy Mary of Refugio," calls a voice through the cracks in the hut.

"Conceived without sin," answers the *Prencipal*.

The tiny door opens. A dog growls. A cloud of stifling smoke greets the newcomers as they go inside; they hold their hats in their hands, and bow to the right and to the left.

At the rear of the hut the girl—the reason for this ceremonial pilgrimage—is making tortillas. Her face, red from the heat of the fire, hides her perturbation a little, because she is as fidgety as a newly caged turtle dove, but finally she grows calm at the thought of the future that the old ones are so caringly preparing for her.

By the door her father, Mateo Bautista, looks at the newcomers, expressionless. Bibiana Petra, his wife, plump and healthy, does not conceal her happiness and indicates two stones for the visitors to sit on.

"Do you know why we've come?" the *Prencipal* asks, following the customary formula.

"No," answers Mateo Bautista, lying shamelessly. "But in any case, my poor home is happy with your visit."

"Well, Mateo Bautista, our neighbor and relative here, Juan Lucas, is asking for your daughter so she can warm the *tapexco*—the bed—for his son."

"That answer isn't a bad one... But I don't want my good neighbor Juan Lucas to be sorry some day in the future: my little girl is lazy, she's stubborn and she's not bright in the head... Dark as they come and flat-faced, beauty didn't hand her anything... To tell the truth, I don't know what you could see in her..."

"I haven't had the intelligence," puts in Juan Lucas, "to give my son better luck either... He's being foolish when he wants to cut such a fresh, sweet-smelling little flower for himself. But the truth is, the poor fellow has gone dotty in the head, and my duty as a father is, well..."

In a corner of the impoverished hut Bibiana Petra smiles at how well things are going; there will be a wedding: the way the fathers are so vehemently disparaging their mutual offspring shows this with absolute clarity.

"The thing is, decency doesn't allow you to see anything good in your children… Youth is noble when it's been brought up properly," says the *Prencipal*, reciting something that he has repeated many times on similar occasions.

Bent over the *metate*—the stone for grinding corn, the girl listens; she is the prize they are playing for in this tournament of words, and yet she hasn't even the right to look directly at any of the participants.

"Look, neighbor, my good friend," adds Juan Lucas, "accept these presents that I'm offering you as proof of my good faith."

And Mateo Bautista, with great dignity, repeats the customary phrases for special occasions like these.

"It's not good manners, friend, to accept gifts in one's home when they're first offered, you know that… God be with you."

The visitors stand. The man of the house has kissed the *Prencipal's* hand and embraced his neighbor, Juan Lucas, affectionately. The two of them go out, burdened with the presents that extreme Tzeltal etiquette has prevented the good Mateo Bautista from accepting.

Old Bibiana Petra is bursting with happiness: the first act has turned out splendidly.

With the back of her hand, the girl brushes away the lock of hair fallen over her forehead, and hurries to finish slapping out the mass of dough piling up at one side of the pan.

Silently, Mateo Bautista has squatted down at the door of his hut.

"Bibiana," he orders, "bring me a drink of *guaro*."

The red-faced woman obeys and places a jug of rum in her husband's hands. He begins to drink slowly, savoring each swallow.

The following week the interview again takes place. On this occasion the visitors and the visited are supposed to drink a good amount of *guaro*, and this they do… But the request, made once again, is not accepted, and the presents—enriched now with perfumed soaps, cakes of brown-sugar, and a bag of salt—are again refused. The men do not speak much this time; it is simply that words lose their eloquence before indefatigable protocol.

The girl has stopped going to the river for water—the customary ritual is thus established—but the boy does not leave off touching the suggestive roundness of the vessels, rhythmically, with his hands.

On the third visit Mateo Bautista must give in gracefully… And so he does: then he accepts the gifts with a peevish expression, despite the fact that they have been increased with an undergarment of wool, a *huipil*-blouse embroidered with silk flowers and butterflies, earrings, a necklace made of wire and a nuptial ring, all of them presents from the groom to his future bride.

They speak about dates and groomsmen. The old ones arrange everything with the greatest possible tact.

The girl continues to grind corn on the *metate*; her face, inflamed by the irreverent embers, is impassive. She listens in silence to the plans, not allowing her hands to rest: she grinds and slaps out dough, she slaps out dough and grinds, morning till night.

It is nearly dawn. Bibiana Petra and her daughter have spent a sleepless night. The neighbor women have come to the grinding for the wedding, and they surround the bride, whose duty it is to grind the twelve-pound sack of corn and slap out the hundreds of tortillas that will be consumed during the wedding feast. The dark *mole* boils in large pots. Mateo Bautista has arrived with two large jugs of *guaro*, and the house, the dirt floor swept and dampened, awaits the arrival of the groom's retinue.

Now they are here. For the first time he and she stand close and look at each other. The girl smiles, demure and timid; he becomes serious and lowers his head while cuffing the ground with his creaking-new *guarache*-sandals.

The *Prencipal* has stepped into the middle of the hut. Bibiana Petra is spreading rose petals over the floor. The wooden flute squawks loudly as the guests invade the space.

Now the couple is kneeling humbly at the *Prencipal's* feet. Everyone gathers around them. The *Prencipal* talks about the rights of man and the submission of woman… about the orders he will give and the obedience she must show. He has the bride and groom hold hands, and prays the Lord's Prayer with them... The bride stands and goes to her father-in-law—Juan Lucas, Tzeltal Indian from Bachajón—and kisses his feet. He raises her politely, with dignity, and hands her to his son.

And finally, Bibiana Petra moves into action... Her role is brief, but interesting.

"She is your wife," she says solemnly to the son-in-law... "When you wish, you may take her to your house so that she can warm the *tapexco*, the bed, for you."

Then the young man replies with the sacred phrase:

"Very well, Mother, since you wish it..."

The couple goes out slowly and humbly. She walks behind him like a small lamb.

Bibiana Petra, no longer following protocol, weeps tenderly and says:

"The girl is content... My daughter is very content, because this is the happiest day of her life. Our men will never know how pleasing it is for us women to change our *metate*..."

As they turn through the thorny valley, his hand grasps her plump little finger, and they listen, starry-eyed, to the trill of a linnet.

# THE COWS OF QUIVIQUINTA 〰

The dogs of Quiviquinta were going hungry. The dogs of Quiviquinta roamed about, their backs arched and their noses burrowing into the ruts of back roads, eyes alert, teeth bared. They roved in packs, baying at the moon, snarling at the sun, because the dogs of Quiviquinta were hungry...

And the men, the women and the children of Quiviquinta were hungry too. The grain in the troughs was gone now, the cheese in the hurdles had been eaten, not even a strip of beef hung from the meat-hooks ...

Yes, there was hunger in Quiviquinta; the maize fields turned yellow before the corn could sprout, and the water formed into puddles at the roots of shrubs; water from the clouds, and water that fell from the eyes in the form of tears.

In the huts of the Coras the perpetual hand-slapping of the women had become silent; there was no reason now because, without corn, there was no *nixtamal*, no cooked corn, and with no *nixtamal* there was no dough, and without this, well, there weren't any tortillas either, and since there were no tortillas, it followed that the perpetual sound of hand-slapping of the women had become silent in the huts of the Coras.

Black barley cakes were cooking in the pans now. Black cakes that the people ate, knowing all the while that cramps, the precursor of diarrhea or the runs, were lying in wait for them.

"Eat, child, but don't drink water," the women counseled.

"Barley tortillas are no food for Christians: barley brings chills," warned the old men as they lifted the unpleasant sop grudgingly to their mouths.

"The bad part is that for this comin' year we won't even have no seeds," said Esteban Luna, a handsome, young man who sat near the hearth at this moment, gazing at his wife, Martina. She was also young, slightly plump, but attractive and healthy, and she was smiling at her daughter's caresses: she was a tiny, little thing, her lips and small hands clutching at a fleshy, abundant, dark breast as though it were a small earthen jug.

"She's lucky," remarked Esteban. "She has plenty to eat and a good place to get it from."

Martina laughed agreeably, and stroked the smooth little head of the child as it nursed.

"That's true, but I'm afraid she'll get sick to the stomach. Barley isn't good for little ones…"

Esteban looked at his wife and at his daughter with sad eyes.

"A year ago," he reflected, "I didn't have anything or anyone to worry about… Now, things have gotten worse, there's three of us… And hunger is closing in on us like wildfire."

Martina pretended not to listen to her husband's words. She got to her feet and carried her daughter to the cradle that was suspended from the ceiling of the hut. There she covered her, attentively and tenderly. Esteban remained where he was, taciturn, vaguely regarding the sparks as they flew from the empty fireplace, from the useless hearth.

"Tomorrow I'll go over to Acaponeta and try to find work…"

"No, Esteban," she protested. "What would we do without you?"

"We've got to eat, Martina… Yes, tomorrow I'm off to Acaponeta or to Tuxpan to find work as a laborer or a servant, or whatever I can get."

At the doorway to their hut, their friend, Evaristo Rocha, overheard Esteban's words.

"That way's closed off to us now, brother," announced the visitor. "Jesús Trejo and Madaleno Rivera just got back from the north, and they're starving to death, even worse than we are... According to them, there's no work anywhere; the land is flooded all the way to Escuinapa and even further on... Imagine!"

"Then... What can we do?" asked Esteban Luna in alarm.

"Well, who knows...! Some say they'll send corn from Jalisco. But I don't hardly believe that... How can they make them go hungry over there just so we can have a bite to eat?"

"Right now I don't care if they send us corn or not; we're getting by on barley, mesquite, nopal and pineapple... But when the dry season comes, what will we eat then?"

"That's a good question... But we won't solve anything by leaving the village; we ought to stay here... Especially you, Esteban Luna: you got folks to take care of."

"The only people doing all right here, Evaristo, are the ones who've got animals; we already cooked the rooster... The hens are walking around out there, widows, keeping themselves alive on stinkbugs, earthworms and crickets; the little dirt-egg they lay, that's for Martina; she's nursing and we got to feed her any way we can."

"Don Remigio, the bearded one, he's selling milk at twenty *centavos* a pint."

"That old bandit...! Have you ever heard the like? Today, more than ever, I'm sorry I sold our little cow... Right about now she'd have had her calf and would be giving milk... What the devil did we sell her for, Martina?"

"What do you mean, 'what for,' you Christian...! Have you forgotten already? To fit ourselves out with farm-tools for a year. Didn't you buy a hoe? Didn't you rent two oxen? And the workers you paid to clear the corn fields?"

"Well today, I swear to God, I could hit myself for being so stupid."

"Crying won't do any good, Esteban... We'll just have to make do for a while, and see what God's will is!" added Evaristo Rocha in resignation.

It is Thursday, market-day in Quiviquinta. Esteban and Martina, their bodies and clothing sparkling-clean, go to the marketplace, following custom more than carried along by necessity, moved more by habit than by the offerings that the squalid, nearly vacant *tianguis*, the marketplace, presents to them. Here the indigence and disaster of the area are visible: a few stands with withered, dried-up vegetables; a table holding smelly viscera covered with flies; a kettle where two or three kilos of skinny pork strips are boiling in front of expectant dogs, sitting on their bony, mangy haunches, licking their chops, hoping in vain for the morsel that the ragged children would like to have for themselves. Those children, dying of hunger, who with their rough horseplay nearly overturn the sad, rickety stands with their peanuts and yellow, withered oranges.

Esteban and Martina walk along the Calle Real of Quiviquinta to the market; he goes in front, carrying a little hen with a red crest; she is holding the baby. Martina is proud of the cap with its embroidered stripes, and the little white gown that covers her daughter's small, brown body.

On the road they run into Evaristo Rocha.

"Are you going shopping…?" their friend asks in greeting.

"Shopping? No, no way; farm life is too poor; we're going to see what there is to see… I'm taking the hen in case I can find a buyer for her… If that happens, then I'll buy this one something in the plaza…"

"All right then… God be with you!"

As they pass the house of Don Remigio, the bearded one, Esteban slows down and looks, without attempting to conceal his envy, at a peon milking an emaciated, melancholic cow that flicks its tail to drive away the cloud of hovering flies.

"The rich are making out all right… Don Remigio's family isn't, and won't be, hungry… They have three cows. Even if things are bad, each of them will give their three liters… Two for drinking, and what's left over, well, to sell… Yes, those people will have a way to do the planting next year; but as for us…"

Martina looks at her man, startled. Then the two of them continue on their way.

Martina strips the bark from a stalk of sugar cane with her short, wide, sparkling white teeth. Esteban watches her silently while he clumsily lulls the baby in his arms who is crying at the top of her lungs.

People come and go through the market place, not even daring to ask the prices of the sparse merchandise that the traders are hawking loudly ... Everything is so expensive!

Esteban stands, waiting. The little hen, tied fast on the loose dirt, flaps its wings.

"How much for the chicken-stew?" a man asks boldly, running an expert hand over the small bird's breast to check the extent and quality of its flesh.

"Four *pesos*," answers Esteban...

"Four *pesos*? Huh! Not even if it was a heifer..."

"That's just so you can make me an offer, man..."

"I'll give you two for her."

"No... What do you think, that I stole her?"

"You won't win, and I won't either... Let's make it twenty *reales*."

"It's not worth it. She's eaten that much in corn."

And the would-be buyer goes off, unconcerned about the failure of the purchase.

"You should have given her to him, Esteban. She's so old, it's hard for her to lay eggs anymore," said Martina.

The baby is still crying. Martina puts aside the sugar cane and takes her daughter from her husband's arms. She pulls her blouse up to her neck and exposes the magisterial, beautiful, dark breasts that tremble like a pair of udders about to burst. The child clings to one of them; Martina, chaste as a Biblical matron, allows her daughter to suckle while her lips hum a lively little tune.

A new sound is added to the buzz of the marketplace: the motor of an approaching automobile. In Quiviquinta, an automobile is a rare sight. Since the town is cut off from the highway, few motorized vehicles dare make their way over the wild, mountainous paths. Shrieking and laughing, a mob of children follows the automobile that arouses everyone's curiosity when it stops near the plaza. A married couple steps out: the man, tall, strong, prosperous in appearance, pride glowing in his face; the woman, small, weakly, with timid movements.

The new arrivals sweep the market place with their eyes; they are looking for something. They walk into the crowd, they turn from one side to another, they make inquiries, and then they go on, intent on their search.

They come to a dead stop before Esteban and Martina who, when she sees the strangers and taken with sudden embarrassment, pulls the blouse down over her breasts. But her actions are too late; the foreigners have already discovered what they needed to know:

"Did you see?" the man asks the woman.

"Yes," she answers excitedly. "That one. I want that one. She's magnificent!"

"She certainly is!" the man exclaims enthusiastically.

Then, without further hesitation, he addresses Martina:

"Look, you, do you want to come with us? We'll take you to Tepic as our wet-nurse, so you can breast-feed our little boy."

The Indian woman stands there, dumbstruck, looking at the couple, not answering.

"Twenty *pesos* a month, good food, a good bed, you'll be treated well…"

"No," answers Esteban drily.

"Don't be a fool, man. You're starving to death, and still you make us beg you," barks the stranger.

"No," Esteban cuts him off again.

"Twenty-five pesos every month. What do ya' say?"

"No."

"All right, let's get this over and done with: fifty *pesos*."

"Will you give seventy-five *pesos*? And take me at just half milk?" Martina proposes unexpectedly.

Esteban looks, unbelieving, at his wife; he wants to speak, but they won't let him.

"Seventy-five *pesos*, and it's all the milk… All right?"

Esteban is left in a daze, and when he tries to get a word in, Martina places her hand over his mouth.

"I want to!" she answers. And then, to her husband, as she hands their daughter to him: "Go on, feed her goat's milk mixed with rice… nothing can hurt poor children. It's her duty, and it's mine too, to help you."

Mechanically, Esteban holds out his hands to take their daughter.

And then, with an expression that tries to be happy, Martina says:

"If Don Remigio, the bearded one, has his cows to get what he needs for next year, you have yours too, Esteban… And yours gives more. We'll plant the whole field next year, I'll get us what we need."

"Let's go," says the stranger nervously, taking the girl's arm.

As Martina climbs into the car, she is crying softly.

The foreign woman tries to comfort her.

"These Cora Indian women," affirms the man, "are known for the quality of their milk…"

The car starts up. The people in the market place cannot take their eyes from it as it leaves.

Esteban cries out to Martina. His shouts are lost in all the commotion.

Then he takes the road back to his house. He doesn't

turn his head, he trudges along slowly, dragging his feet… Under his arms, the hen, and held close to his chest, the child, who whimpers, having lost her two small jugs of dark clay.

# Hiculi Hualula  ⌒⟩

"**I**t was the UNCLE, it was the... the uncle," moaned the woman, her glassy eyes fixed on the face of the cadaver that had once been a robust, young man. The patriarch of Tezompan stood before her, solemn and stern, listening.

The woman, caught up in a frenzy of hysterical chattering, could not hold her tongue:

"He came home last night, drunk... He was saying terrible things; then he questioned the truth of the uncle more than three times. Finally, stiff with *mescal*, he fell asleep. This morning he was dead... what happened was he provoked him, yes, more than three times he questioned the power of the uncle, the one whose name only you, the oldest and wisest, can say aloud."

The patriarch was silent for a few moments while the woman looked at him expectantly. Then, slowly and clearly, he spoke the word forbidden to all lips but his own:

"When he is provoked, Hículi Hualula is perverse, vengeful, evil; but, on the other hand.."

The old man cut off the sentence he had barely begun, perhaps because he remembered that I was present, I, an outsider who had come a week earlier to badger the reserved Huichola people of Tezompan with my impertinent questions as an ethnologist... But it was too late now; the strange word was written down in my notebook; there it was: Hículi Hualula, an unexpected expression that only the oldest and wisest man was permitted to speak.

The patriarch glanced at me in distrust. He realized that he had committed a serious indiscretion, and he tried to correct his blunder while at the same time taking care not to break the immutable laws of hospitality. Then the old man spoke a few words to the woman in the Indian tongue. She turned toward me, staring with her tiny, reddish eyes, and let loose a stream of words in Huichol, that rigid language of exotic sounds that I had only heard briefly at erudite discourses of philologists... When she had finished her tirade, the new widow, overcome with tears, threw herself onto the dead man's chest, and broke into emotional weeping and heaving.

The old patriarch stroked the woman's head tenderly. Then he approached me and very courteously said:

"It's best for us to leave her with only her pain for company."

He took me by the arm, and with a kind expression, guided me to the door of the hut; but I stopped, stubbornly. I couldn't leave without delving into the enigma of the words in my notebook, insistently demanding my professional attention.

"What is Hículi Hualula?" I asked quickly and drily.

The old man let go my arm and took a step backward. His eyes flashed, and his lips turned surly:

"For your own well-being, sir, don't repeat those words. Only I can speak them without incurring his anger."

"I need to know who he is, what abilities and powers he has."

The man did not speak another word; he stood there inflexibly, his eyes sunken and empty, as though looking inside himself the way melancholy, ancestral deities do...

It was useless to insist; the man had withdrawn into himself in pointed silence, but it was so pained that I decided to abandon that path of investigation, more out of pity than fear. And yet, from that moment I believed that I was more deeply bound than ever to delve into the very depths of the enigma.

Then I realized that only by uncovering the mystery behind

the evil expression would my project be a complete success, and that not knowing it would mean nothing less than failure.

This explains very well the obsession to which I fell victim for several days. Being certain that a direct investigation would be useless, would perhaps have adverse effects, I decided to work my way around the unknown with a series of discreet inquiries, whose conclusions, judiciously woven together, could give me more satisfactory results...

But one morning, when the scorching intensity of the recurring hot spells had hammered at me more severely than usual, my moderation fell apart, and once again I found myself hurling down the path of indiscretion. Doña Lucía, the half-breed, was preparing a medicinal drink, *quina*, in my honor; next to her three or four Huichol women were busy at the domestic hearths, pulverizing roasted corn for the beverage. When Doña Lucía, plump and good-natured, held out the jug with the bitter mixture to me, the irrepressible, brusque question came to my lips:

"Doña Lucía, do you know what or who Hículi Hualula is?"

The woman shrunk back in fright, she put her index finger to her lips, and unable to breathe, glanced over at the Indian women who covered their ears, and in terrible consternation, ran, horrified, from the hut.

The half-breed, showing signs of great uneasiness, took my right hand between her own plump hands, and, with a tone more of commiseration than reproach, said to me:

"Please, sir, never say those words... Now you've done me a great harm, my servants have left and they won't come back to this house where the name of the uncle has been vilely spoken until the light of the new moon breaks the spell."

"You know, Doña Lucía. Tell me who it is, what it is, where it is..."

Without another word, the woman turned her back to me; then she bent over the *metate*, the grinding stone, and set herself to doing the work the Hucholas had left unfinished.

That same afternoon I had to go to a seed-planting, to write down the words of a farming ballad in Huichol. The farmer who was going to recite the words of the song for me was waiting, leaning against a barbed wire fence that protected his work. The beautiful corn field was his: tall, thick, dark-green stalks of corn quivered with the passing of a warm breeze; the man felt proud, his good will was obvious. Here we had an Indian, small and dry as a reed of tall grass. He spoke very little, but smiled a great deal; you could say that he lost no opportunity to display his magnificent set of teeth.

"A nice field of corn, Catarino," I greeted him.

"Yes it's nice," he answered.

"Did you put compost on the land?"

"I didn't have to, it's good all by itself… and with the help of God and the uncle, the stalks will grow, they'll bloom and they'll make a lot of nice little corn," he said in a simple tone, the way people say adages, common maxims, or public prayers.

I felt a tingling sensation in my body: I was about to commit another foolish act.

"Did you say the uncle?" I asked with exaggerated indifference. "The one whose name cannot be spoken aloud?"

"Yes" Catarino answered simply. "The uncle is good to everyone who respects him."

In the Huichol's face there was such serenity, and in his words there was so much trust and faith, that just the thought of wresting the secret from him gave me a perverse feeling.

Anyway, that afternoon I made some slight progress in uncovering the mystery: the uncle was good when he granted life, but the uncle was bad when he brought death.

It didn't take me long to jot down the words of the sowing song. I thanked Catarino for his kindness and headed back to Tezompan.

On the way I ran into Mateo San Juan, the country schoolteacher. He was a good boy: a pure-blooded Huichol. His intelligence was obvious in the first words we exchanged; I could also see the young man's desire to better the economic and cultural condition of his people. Mateo was especially interested in telling outsiders that he had lived and studied in Mexico City, in the Native Students' House, during the time of Mexico's former president, Calles.

Mateo San Juan was accessible and communicative. Having finished his teaching chores early, he was taking a walk that afternoon. In his hands there rolled a beautiful piece of fruit, a *chirimoya*. When he saw me, he broke the fruit in two, and graciously offered me half. We walked along together, savoring the sweetness of the *chirimoya*, and the no less pleasant company.

And yet, I was not faithful to Mateo San Juan: everything I said was aimed at guiding the conversation toward my own interests. It wasn't that difficult to get to the heart of the matter; Mateo himself opened the door for it when he began to talk about all the difficulties an outsider faced before he could probe the reality of the Indians: "It's easier for us to understand your world than it is for city people to come to know our simple minds," said Mateo San Juan, rather proud of his statement.

"What is Hículi Hualula?" I asked boldly.

Mateo San Juan looked at me serenely, and I even noticed a certain ironic curl to his lips.

"It's not strange that the mystery has you under its spell: the same thing happens to every outsider who probes its existence... I would advise you to be very discreet when you talk about it, if you want to avoid unpleasant repercussions."

"That's what I thought, but I won't rest until I get to the bottom of it... You would be an ideal informant, Mateo San Juan," I said, somewhat perturbed by the teacher's attitude.

"Don't expect me to shed any light on the uncle... Have a good day, Mr. Investigator." And with that, he hurried on ahead until he was running at a little trot.

"Say, Mateo, wait," I shouted a number of times, but the country school teacher didn't stop, and finally, at a bend in the road, he disappeared from sight.

Saturday came, and with it my only hope; the priest from Colotlán was in Tezompan, making the weekly rounds of his parish. When the old priest dismounted from his gray mule, and before he could take off his cloth duster, I was already at his side, begging him to listen to me for a few brief moments. The clergyman courteously placed himself at my disposal.

"Look," I said, "I need to talk to you in complete privacy."

"All right," answered the priest, "we can be alone in the sacristy as long as we need to."

And there, in those silent surroundings, the priest told me everything he had been able to discover about the uncle.

"The truth is," he said, "that question piqued my interest long ago, but the reserve of these people never allowed me to delve as deeply as I would have liked into that mysterious obsession. They call him uncle because they imagine he's the brother of father God, *tata* God, and to them he's so powerful that the entire village can sleep easily if they know they're under his protection... But the uncle is cruel and vengeful, anyone who insults him or says his name aloud will pay with his life...

"That is reserved for only the eldest in the community. Under the protection of the uncle, the Huicholes make their journeys without being afraid. They think that with his influence, serpents will leave the road, lightning will strike only at a distance, and all their enemies will be powerless. No illness can resist the uncle, and the only men who die are the ones who are not in his good graces... I'm sorry, my friend," concluded the clergyman, "that I can't give you any more precise information, because now my efforts are concentrated less on learning the details about that devilish belief than in tearing it from the hearts of these poor people..."

"All right," I said to myself when I was alone, weighing the information the priest had provided me with, "what little I know about the uncle is hardly even an incentive for me to dig more deeply into the mystery and make something clear and concrete of it..." I found that my investigation of the Huicholes was coming to an end; in two days I needed to be with the Coras, and I would have to give up my search for the unknown, perhaps forever.

A timid knock at the door interrupted my soliloquy. Without waiting to be invited, Mateo San Juan entered the hut that served both as my living quarters and my laboratory. At that moment the country teacher wore a comically enigmatic expression; he was wrapped in a bright reddish-purple blanket that covered him all the way up to his chin, while the brim of his straw hat fell over his eyes. When he greeted me there was a slight trembling in his voice. His demeanor made me feel that something important was about to happen. Mateo remained standing even though I cordially invited him to sit down on one of the rustic benches that furnished my hut.

"I've thought a long time about what I've come here to do. I've weighed the step I'm about to take, because I don't want to be selfish. The entire world, not only the Huicholes, should enjoy the benefits of the uncle, enjoy its effects and appreciate all its blessings…"

"Then, are you willing to…?"

"Yes, even though what I'm going to reveal means risking my own skin."

"I don't think, Mateo San Juan, that someone who's a country schoolteacher should have superstitious fears, the way common natives do."

"I'm not afraid of the uncle,—it's his nephews that scare me. But let me repeat, I don't want to be selfish; all humanity should be able to benefit from the powers of the uncle…"

"Let's get to the point, if you don't mind, and cut out the preliminaries."

"When science," continued Mateo, without changing his tone, "uses the uncle in its service, then all men, the same as we Huicholes, will have found real happiness in life; they will no longer suffer physical pain, their weariness will come to an end; their passion for health will be magnified while a luminous dream lifts them to paradise; their thirst will be quenched without drinking, their hunger without eating, they will feel a rebirth of strength everyday, and no task will be too difficult for them… I know that the science of the microscope, of chemistry with all its reactions, will accomplish wonders on that day when the gifts of the uncle are put within the grasp of everyone… The uncle that stimulates friendship and love, a gentle narcotic, a wise counselor; and with its aid men will become better, because nothing will unite them but mutual happiness and complete understanding. The uncle makes the heart tender, the head light…"

"Stop right there," I interrupted him in disillusionment, "the uncle is nothing more than *peyote*. Isn't it?"

Mateo San Juan smiled disdainfully and said:

"You people have known about *peyote* for years, its effects are common, intoxicating, fleeting, and for that reason they're more dangerous than they are beneficial… The uncle is very different; until now, no one, except we Huicholes, has experienced its extraordinary gifts…"

"All right… How can I get the uncle to the laboratories in Mexico City?"

Mateo San Juan turned solemnly, and drawing apart his poncho, he put a small, light package, no larger than a man's fist, into my hands.

"Here it is… Take it. Some day all men will praise its virtues, it will be more highly valued than wealth, it will be as useful as bread, as prized as love and as desirable as health. It is wrapped in leaves from the aloe, the only ones resistant to its strong secretions. Don't open it until the very moment when it's ready to be studied, and make certain that that's done within the week… Ah, if my people discover that I've just delivered it into the hands of an outsider, they'll kill me…! Go, today. Take it, and don't forget your friend, Mateo San Juan."

"Thank you, but how could your countrymen make such terrible accusations against you if the uncle brings only good thoughts and noble actions?"

The rural school teacher said soberly:

"They would never forgive me because the Huicholes look on him as the brother of the unapproachable divinity. You people, on the other hand, will know only about its beneficial effects, and you will esteem it simply for itself… Take it and put it to good use, but go immediately, before time hides all its virtues from the laboratories."

"I'm not going to Mexico City right away," I informed him, "but this very afternoon my assistant will take the uncle with him to Colotlán, and he'll send it on to Mexico City by registered mail, along with a letter of mine, to the Biological Institute, where they'll examine it and study it closely."

"I hope everything works out well, Mr. Investigator."

"Thank you again, Mateo San Juan. You've done a very good thing."

That same afternoon, in accordance with our plans, my assistant, a young half-breed from Colotlán, left with instructions to send the uncle very safely by mail. I was supposed to leave a little later for the lands of the Cora Indians where I would make a quick stop to review certain information we weren't certain about… But first I wanted to say good-bye to the good country school teacher.

I went to his hut. A little, old Indian woman, humble and frightened, was at his door, surrounded by neighbor women who were consoling her. When she saw me, she spoke with a trembling, choked voice:

"It was the uncle... yes, it was the uncle who does not forgive..."

With great trepidation, I went into the hut. There, stretched out on a mat of palm leaves was my friend, Mateo San Juan. His face beaten to a pulp, and his body pounded with clubs, filled me with pity. He crinkled his misshapen face to welcome me with a smile:

"The poor women," he said. "They think it was the uncle, but it was his nephews, just as I feared."

When I returned to Mexico City, I first visited the Institute of Biology. There they knew nothing about the uncle, since they had received no package from me in the mail. Then I inquired at the post office, and the results were also negative. The next step was to write a letter to my assistant in Colotlán. I waited a couple weeks for his answer. When I received none, I pressed the matter with a telegram. This did bring a reply: in an anguished and very cowardly missive, he begged me dramatically to never again mention anything to him "regarding what your worthy letter deals with," because what he had been through on account of my visit "was nearly fatal for the undersigned."

Lacking an assistant, I wrote to Mateo San Juan. The letter was returned to me, unopened. I sent another, and the results were identical to the first.

The priest in Colotlán was my last hope. I wrote to him in complete confidentiality; I openly told him everything, and earnestly begged him to send me the Hículi Hualula again. A few days later I received a brief letter from the priest: Mateo, pressured by the people of his village, had left the region and hired himself out as a *bracero*; the last they had heard of him was that he was in Oklahoma, working on the railway... "And in regard to your small request," continued the priest's letter, "I'm truly sorry that I can't help you, but it would bring about immediate calamities, rows and tension that my ministry is here to prevent, rather than provoke. As for your plans for making another trip to these latitudes, I advise you, if you value your life, not even to attempt it."

For me, my failure has been maddening, my anxiety has developed into a mania. This has brought on hallucinations, and the hal-

lucinations have taken on alarming manifestations... I have seen him
in dreams, yes, dressed in the sumptuous garments the Huicholes
wear in the ceremony for the Father Sun... He has passed by me and
winked his eye; when I called him by name, Hículi Hualula laughed
loudly and harshly, spitting out reddish gobs of sputum at my feet.

It was a magnificent afternoon when I found him directing
traffic at the intersection of Juárez Avenue and San Juan de Letrán:
his merciless face, stony, a turquoise ring through his lower lip, on
his head a crest of macaw feathers, his feet in golden sandals, and his
horrid index finger, the flesh composed of green nopal, wielding an
agave skewer as a fingernail, pointed at me, while ghastly curses in
Huichol slid from his mouth...

Someone told me that whoever took me to the Red Cross heard
me say these words:

"The uncle... it was the uncle who never forgives," while at the
same time my eyes were rolling idiotically... That I was completely
helpless, and my pulse was rapid...

The doctor prescribed bromides, rest and warm baths...

# THE MOCKING BIRD AND THE FOOTPATH  ⤳

It happened among the Chinantecos, those small, reserved and charmingly discourteous Indians. It happened among them, in their own nest that fell behind the mountain of Ixtlán de Juárez, in the very foothills of that extraordinary wonder of our Mexican orography they call the Knot of Cempoaltépetl.

We chose Yólox—San Marcos Yólox, to be precise—as the ideal place for setting up our anthropological laboratory… Yólox is a municipality of scarcely three hundred inhabitants, clinging to the side of the mountain, surrounded by sunflowers and agave plants. Around Yólox—a pleasant name meaning heart in the Aztec tongue—lie ranches, communities, and clusters of huts, from which the Indians come down every Friday, ready to play their dual role of buyers and sellers in the market place, a commerce of animated and picturesque bartering: salt, for grain; quarry from the hunt or small animals from the river or lake, in exchange for cuttings of course wool; herbal medicines, for strips of soles for *huarache*-sandals; agave fiber wound into crude skeins, traded for tallow candles; chickens, for hanks of yarn…

We took over the abandoned little schoolhouse there, and set up our technical equipment. It was our job to validate a theory, born from the writing desk of a reputed European expert, with irrefutable statistical data. In other words, we investigators were to sew up the loose ends of science—a role similar to that of the shoemaker who puts the shine to a pair of old boots. Or, to put it more simply, in our hands we held a compass, and it was our job to manufacture a suitable collection of directions for it; otherwise the brilliant hypothesis of the professor would give up the ghost at the very instant it was beginning to gain prestige in lecture halls, and credence in academies.

A week went by and we began to feel uneasy. The Europeans who made up part of the expedition were protesting:

"All right then," they argued, "if these Indians refuse to let us study them, let's do what we did in Eritrea and Azerbaijan: bring them in by force, at the point of a bayonet if we have to..."

We Mexicans, who understand our land, trembled just thinking what an act of violence could do to the volatile Chinantecos.

We made some progress on Saturday: a drunken beggar agreed to let us study him. Then our nickel-plated instruments were put to work: the anthropometer, the compasses, the dynamometer and the platform-scale. There were blood tests, and even an attempt to measure basal metabolism.

After our success in analyzing the first case, and when that case left the laboratory with a decent amount of change, we noticed an improved understanding among the subjects who followed and even some sympathy toward us.

But things became seriously complicated when something unexpected happened—something never before written in the centurial annals of Yólox: its sky, serene yesterday, was startled by the shudder of a motor, its blue vilely stained by a gray, smoking contrail... An airplane had flown overhead!

There was terrible fright among the Indians; the women wrapped their arms tightly around their babies as their eyes followed the trajectory of the brilliant bird... The men grabbed hold of their slings and their guns; someone shot twice at the inexorable traveler as it flew in a southerly direction; a strong, young man boldly climbed to the top of a tree. Afterward he claimed to have seen the bird's beak and enormous claws holding onto a struggling young ox...

When the unwanted visitor became lost in the clouds and in the distance, the Indians, shaken with terror, came to us. Then we saw that the place we had chosen for our work wasn't large enough: the entire town packed its way inside. Someone asked us, in a halting tongue, about those fantastic sparrow-hawks. While we could very well have used those moments of fear to further our work, we forgot about the probable advantages and instead used an uncertain means that was much more truthful and honorable:

"It's a mechanical device that flies," I said. "It's like a stone, launched from a slingshot... Men, just like you and like us, ride in it."

"Are you saying that there are men inside the belly of that bird?" the Indian turned to inquire.

"No, not exactly, because what you're calling a bird is nothing but a machine..."

The interpreter, a hard, serious old man, playing his role to the hilt as the greatest authority in the village, stared at me incredulously, but he repeated my words in his own language. Then there was an expectant silence.

"Look," he argued, "a stone goes up a distance, and then it comes back down... But that big bird flies on and on, using its wings."

"The fact is," I answered, "that machine has the ingredients of fire in its belly: gasoline, oil, grease..."

The old man's mouth twisted in a suspicious smile:

"Don't take us for stupid people... You must think we're nothin' but fools."

Then, in his monosyllabic language, he spoke drawn-out, solemn words. No sooner had he finished than the crowd left our laboratory. Some, especially the women, spilled out in a violent rush, others looked at us with frightened, malevolent eyes as they went out.

We were left with only a small, sad, sickly, worn-down group of people. You might say that the weight of their misery and illness held them there, nailed them to the spot. It was a family of three: the father, feeble and dull, bared his uneven, horribly crooked teeth as he smiled; the mother, small, with flabby, purplish skin, showed signs of advanced pregnancy; the daughter, a girl who had been surprised—snatched away—by puberty, with no time to exchange the sadness, the infantile gentleness of her Mongoloid eyes for the brightness that lights up the young, no time to convert her linear form into the softness of flowering youth.

"Sick, we be sick… real sick, dear *patrón*," said the man, pointing to his family.

With such obvious symptoms the diagnosis was easy: they were all suffering from malaria. That was what their disfigured appearance, their weak grimaces, their swollen, yellowish arms and legs cried out to us.

"We be sick… real sick, *patrones*," repeated the Indian in a wailing tone.

But, more than sick, for us these miserable people were subjects to be studied, perhaps the tangible evidence, born in remote climes, of a theory that needed the compost of statistics, the fertilization of arithmetical figures… they were numbers, for us to make use of.

The scientific instruments reappeared, bewildering them. We measured their stature and volume, the size of their bones, the shape of the cranium, their weight, and the coagulative quality of their blood. In wonder, fear reeling in their eyelids, they let us do as we wished, certain that our actions would restore them to health.

After we had filled in the answers to complicated questions, we let them rest.

The man said a few words to his family, then he took my hand to kiss it. The women tried to do the same. Filled with shame, I declined that display of gratitude. I felt guilty of being deceitful and of telling lies, of resorting to unscrupulous methods, even if, under the circumstances, it was necessary … Then I remembered something in our first-aid kit that might give some relief to the pain of these poor people. I found a bottle of quinine tablets. I filled the cupped hands that were held out to me, trembling, like thirsty little birds, with those beautiful granules, scarlet and shiny, like peonies. I ran my hand over the little girl's cheek, and let them leave. As she went out the door, the woman smiled at us sadly, in pain…

In the small plaza the inhabitants of Yólox were talking, arguing, their voices reaching a feverish pitch, looking up at the sky and shaking their fists.

When the family with malaria crossed the plaza, everyone made way, more afraid of being contaminated by their contact with us, than by any illness; their eyes showed compassion and good will. They lowered their voices until they were nearly mute. The sick ones passed through the crowd without stopping; they were going back to their low land, where lethal malaria rages.

My friends, the Europeans, were growing desperate. It was essential for us to convince the Chinantecos, or force them if necessary, to give themselves over to our experiment; since I knew those people best, I opted for finding an amicable way. I went to see the old interpreter. I was completely certain that not only was he the sole man in the village who understood Spanish, but that with his practice of magic and witchcraft he had a decisive influence over his people. His position among the Chinantecos was based on civil authority, which was nothing more than a way for him to reinforce his power. I found him in his hut. The submissiveness he had shown—during the moments of terror brought about by the airplane in the Chinantla skies—had turned now to a haughty, defensive, caustic attitude. For me he had clipped, conventional phrases, just as the Indians' inbred hospitality required, but in his expression there were misgivings and deep animosity.

I spoke at length, for perhaps ten or fifteen minutes, and when I thought I had convinced the sphinx, as though my words had glanced off his narrow, reserved forehead, he said:

"My people, they know what is happening…, and instead of allowing your plans to be carried out, we will give you two hours to leave the village… If you disobey, we wouldn't give two cents for any of your lives. My advice for you is to saddle your animals and get out of here before the morning star is in the sky… You hear?"

"But," I argued, "we're not here to do anything bad."

"That's what everyone says," replied the old man. "You're all businessmen. Yesterday you traded in cattle and pigs, nowadays you trade in Christians. The men with you are *gringos*, and they feed Christian fat to that brood of giant birds they own… Now they want to carry off the fat of Chinantecos to fill the beaks of those giant hawks… Tell the truth…! We're not so stupid that we don't know what's happening. If they weigh us, if they measure us, if they take our blood… What does it mean? That they think of us as pigs to fatten… But if you want to stay, just you alone," he added in a confidential tone, "tell me, and nobody else, where I can get the eggs of those big birds so I can breed them. I could raise big, beautiful ones in these mountains: they could eat grass, acorns and pinions the way turkeys do… But if you refuse, the morning star will be there to light your road. You understand?"

We didn't wait for the morning star; we left under cover of darkness, at full gallop, in ignominious flight. Rocks flew at our backs, insults and curses rained down.

As we reached the peak, and before our descent to the port of María Andrea, a glorious dawn burst upon us. The pines raised their branches trembling with dew; the striped layers of a strange geological formation marked our route. A variety of shades of verdure—from dark purple to gold—met our eyes. The smell of resin, the song of the wind that brushed branches and was cut on the edge of rocks, the trill of the mocking bird, soothing elements—all of them, themes of quietude, restoratives of faith, calmed our spirits, but they weren't enough to make us forget our humiliation.

One cursed the Indians:

"They're ungrateful, treacherous."

Another came weakly to their defense:

"They've suffered so much: it's only reasonable that they would distrust and fear us."

But the true explanation for those illogical actions, for that absurd situation, awaited us at a turn in the path. There, with faces wasting and haggard, but with expressions of happiness and a display of gaiety, the sick family was waiting for us, the ones to whom we had given quinine tablets. The dull-witted man and the pregnant woman tried once more to kiss our hands, and the little girl stood on tiptoe, to touch us.

We halted the animals for a few moments, and I spoke to them:

"How are you folks? Did you take the medicine?"

The father stood silent, trying to find the right words:

"Yes, we're feeling better…"

"Do you have any pills left?"

In reply, the little man tugged at his shirt collar to show us a necklace of shiny, red quinine tablets.

The woman did the same, and so did the little girl.

"The sickness doesn't come near us any more," said the man, "it's afraid of the string of miraculous stones."

The eyes of the Chinantecos gleamed with a conviction very close to faith.

After that, no one spoke of the ingratitude of the Indians; or of their brutality, or of their discourtesy... There were curses and insults, yes, but not for the Chinantecos, or the Mixes, or for the Coras, or the Seris, or the Yaquis... They were for those men and those systems that, as they chain the fists and shackle the legs, impair the minds, dull the understanding and frustrate the will, with more anger, with more rage than malaria, than tuberculosis, than enterocolitis, than onchocercosis... And the pines, the mocking bird and the footpath all nodded together, in one accord.

# The Parable of The One-Eyed Boy

"...And they lived happily for many years afterward." For as many years as his deformity caught no one's attention. He gave little importance, himself, to the darkness that took away half his sight. From the time he was a little boy he had been aware of his disfigurement, but he resigned himself philosophically: "As long as I've got one good eye, that's all I need." And that was how he kept himself from being bothered by it, to such an extent that he imagined everyone looked on his deformity with the same understanding; because "as long as he had one good one..."

But then came an ill-fated day—when he decided to walk by the school at the very moment the boys and girls were leaving. He held his head high, his step was light; in one hand he carried the basket overflowing with fruit, greens, and vegetables that he was taking to his old clients.

"There goes the one-eyed boy," he heard a small, high-pitched voice say behind him.

The words tumbled around in the silence. There were no other remarks, no laughter, no outcries... It was simply that a discovery had been made.

Yes, a discovery that surprised even him.

"There goes the one-eyed boy... the one-eyed boy... one-eyed," he muttered the whole while it took him to go door to door, making his deliveries.

One-eyed, yes, sir, he finally accepted it. In the mirror that trembled in his hands, a single pupil focused on the cloud obtruding between himself and the sun...

And yet, it could well be that no one would notice the scholar's indiscreet discovery... There were so many one-eyed people in the world! Then it occurred to him—unwisely—to put his optimistic notion to a test.

And so he did.

But as he walked past the front of the school, a terrible weight made him lower his head and suppress the jauntiness of his walk. He avoided any encounter between his orphaned eye and the hundred mocking eyes that followed him, after the taunt "so long, half-light" was uttered.

He stopped, and for the first time he saw the way one-eyed people see: the infantile crowd was a shiny blur in the middle of the street, something without contours, depth, or volume. Then the laughter and the gibes reached his ears with a new tone: he was beginning to hear, the way the one-eyed hear.

From that moment on, life became a torture for him.

The students left their classrooms because their vacation had begun: all the boys and girls scattered throughout the town.

For him, the danger-zone had grown thin: now it was like a spot of oil that oozed down all the streets, through all the plazas... Now the trick of refusing to go past the front of the school didn't work: mortification came out to meet him, unbridled, aggressive. It was the throngs of children that yelled at him in chorus:

*One, two three,*
*one-eye is here...*

Or it was the little twit who, from behind a wall on the street corner, said:

"Hey, you, light your other lamp…"

His reactions began to change: his astonishment turned to grief, his grief to shame, and his shame became rage, because the joke was like an injury to him, and the outcries were a provocation.

In this frame of mind his demeanor began to change too, but it didn't lose that ridiculous aspect, that comical air the children enjoyed so much:

*One, two three,*
*one-eye is here…*

Now he no longer cried; he bit his lip, he bellowed, he cursed, and threatened them with closed fists.

But the taunts continued, and his threats fell on deaf ears.

One day he picked up a handful of stones and threw them, one by one, with evil aim, at the barricade of children who blocked his way. The gang fled, laughing at him. A new nickname was born from this event:

"Sharp-eye".

From that time on there was nothing the throng liked better than to provoke the one-eyed boy.

Of course, one had to take measures against evil things. His doting mother sought remedies from all her friends: cooked mesquite sprouts, rinses with mallow water, poultices of perfumed vinegar…

But nothing held back the remarks:

*One, two three,*
*one-eye is here…*

He caught the little fool by the ear, and shaking with anger, squeezed his throat until his tongue came out. They were at the edge of town, with no witnesses. There he could take his revenge, rising in a frothing mouth and moans… But the unexpected appearance of two men came to prevent the thing that beat like a sublime pleasure in the heart of the one-eyed boy.

He ended up in jail.

The remedies of his mother's friends were forgotten, and she went in search of doctors' prescriptions. Then came salves, eye-drops, plasters, all of which changed the cloud into a thick halo.

The spot of hatred had filtered into unexpected places: one day, as he passed by the pool hall under the arcades, a derelict tried out the taunt:

"So long, sharp-eye…"

And the result was unexpected: one punch by the offended boy caused the big bully to make him pay very dearly for his brazenness… That day the one-eyed boy returned home, bloody and bruised.

He sought a little comfort in his mother's warmth, and some relief for all the bumps on his head in arnica… The old woman softly ran her fingers through the unkempt hair of her son who sobbed at her knees.

Then they thought of looking for another way, not to find a remedy for their troubles, but simply to conceal the deformity that was becoming so painful for them.

Since human measures had failed them, they turned to the divinity for assistance: the mother promised the Virgin of San Juan de los Lagos to take the boy to her sanctuary, bearing a silver eye, an offering they would make to ease the cruelty of all the children.

They decided that he would no longer go into the streets; his mother would take his place in the daily labor of providing fruit, greens and vegetables to the neighbors, an activity they both depended on for their subsistence.

When all was ready for the trip, they entrusted the keys of their little hovel to a neighbor lady, and with full hearts but empty pockets, they began their journey, intent on reaching the altars of miracles on the very days of the festival.

Once inside the sanctuary, they were no more than a dot in the crowd. He was surprised that no one pointed out his deformity. He enjoyed looking at people face to face, walking among them cocksure, making no bones, supported by his insignificance. His mother encouraged him: "You see, the miracle is beginning to work… Blessed be the Virgin of San Juan…!"

And yet, he was never completely convinced of the portent, and he settled simply for enjoying those happy moments, darkened from time to time by the continual ringing in his ears, like a far distant echo, of:

*One, two three,*
*one-eye is here...*

Then wrinkles of grief appeared on his face, along with shadows of rage, and the unpleasant taste of anguish.

It was the day before they were to return. Evening fell as the brotherhoods and groups of pilgrims attended the farewell ceremonies. In the atrium the dancers stamped their feet wildly. The feeble music and the noisemakers joined noise and melody, elevating them like the spirit of a call to prayer. The sky was ablaze; thousands of rockets exploded in a tumult of light, and at the burst of their bellies a surfeit of saltpeter and gunpowder.

At that instant, hypnotized, with his one good eye he followed the trajectory of a huge rocket that was pulling along a rod like a thick tail... At the very moment there was a clap of thunder, a flowering of lights burst out in another part of the sky. His lone eye found pleasure in the ephemeral mixture of colors... Suddenly he felt a terrible blow to his one good eye... Then came darkness, pain, cries.

The crowd gathered around him.

"The tail of a rocket has left my little boy blind," cried the mother, who then begged them: "Get a doctor, for God's sake."

They were going back. His mother was his guide. Painfully, the two of them climbed a steep hill. They had to stop and rest. He moaned and cursed his fate... But as she caressed his face with both her hands, she said:

"My son, I knew that the Virgin of San Juan would not deny us a miracle... Because what she has done for you is clearly a miracle!"

His face turned to bewilderment as he heard these words.

"A miracle, Mother? Well, I'm not grateful to her. I've lost my one good eye at the doors of her temple."

"That's the omen we have to bless her for. When they see you in town they'll all feel cheated, they won't be able to do anything but look for another one-eyed person to make fun of… Because now, my son, you aren't one-eyed any more."

He was silent for a few seconds, then his bitter expression slowly turned to a sweet smile, the smile of a blind man, that lit his entire face.

"It's true, Mother, I'm not one-eyed any more…! Let's come back next year. Yes, let's come back to the Sanctuary and give thanks to Our Lady."

"We'll come back, son, with a pair of silver eyes."

And, slowly, they continued on their way.

# THE REVENGE OF CHARLES LE MANGE ⌐

It was growing late in Chalma, the eve of the Epiphany. Several "companies" of dancers had paraded across the rose-colored tiles covering the floor in the Sanctuary's atrium. In their turn, the Otomís from the plains of Meztitlán performed the barbaric dance of *Los Tocotines* to the sound of drums and reed flutes; the Matlazincas of Ocuilán executed the dance of *The Butterfly and the Flower* with background music of violins and harps; the Pames from San Luis, their faces hidden by terrible masks, adorned with eagle feathers, displayed their brilliant purple and yellow costumes in the dance of *The Conquest*, accompanied by bloodcurdling cries and the loud stomping of *guarache*-sandals. A troop of Aztec girls from Míxquic, all shyness and blushes, presented offerings of flowery ornaments and smoking myrrh incensories to the pale crucified figure. A Tepehua gentleman from the north of Hidalgo, jammed into a jasper frock-coat and wearing a cap of checked cashmere, put his bare feet to the test in a noisy and ridiculous pantomime. For hours at a time the orchestra of Tarascan Indians, brought in from Tzintzuntzan, played *Nana Amalia*, that catchy little tune about love and sighs.

Now that it was growing late in Chalma, now that the magnificent twilight fluttered like a triumphal banner atop Augustinian towers, the Mazahuas of Atlacomulco were on stage. Before the Lord they danced the farce of *The Moors and the Christians* in a descriptive and complicated choreography; they were simulating a battle between the pagans and *The Twelve Peers of France*, and at their head was none other than the *Emperor Charles Le Mange*, all decked out in a cloak and priest's cope trimmed in rabbit skin for want of ermine, a tin crown sprinkled with spangles and tiny pieces of mirror, a kerchief of percale knotted around his neck, and well-worn boots over reddish-purple stockings with white lines, held up with the laces of his bell-bottom pants. To his bare face Charles Le Mange had attached a long beard of golden *ixtle*-fiber, and on his bronze cheeks were two large spots of rouge and a pair of moles painted with burnt pitch-pine.

The rest of the theatrical group was made up of Moors on one side, and Christians on the other. The first were wrapped in cotton caftans, and wore turbans on their heads; their hands wielded wooden cutlasses and scimitars gilded with a banana mixture; the others were elegant knights from Gaul, wearing London-fog sunglasses and draped in cloaks that kicked up at the touch of a sword; velvet caps with plumes of dyed feathers, cloth leggings, and for clogs, creaking, studded *guarache*-sandals.

The attitude and countenance of Charles Le Mange won my sympathy. I followed him in all his evolutions, in his tireless advances and retreats, in his spirited attacks against the infidel, in the arrogant attitude he took when the Christian armies had dispersed all the Moors, and when he recited this quatrain in a thunderous voice:

> *Stay thee, valiant Moor,*
> *Leap thee not the wall,*
> *If Christ thou wouldst behold,*
> *Thou carry still a scar…*

And finally, when the dance was over, dusk now, kneeling, and with his crown in his hands, he prayed fervently to the crucified Christ of Chalma in the center of the Sanctuary nave. Afterward I watched him leave proudly, the blond beard and wig encasing deep, black eyes; his flat, strong nose resting above a handlebar mustache that spilled onto a large mouth, still open, breathing hard from the heated dance that was finished.

My man came out of the church. I could see that his presence impressed his countrymen, the Mazahuas, who were scattered throughout the atrium, just as it did me. Charles Le Mange greeted the crowd with grandiose gestures. A little boy approached the dancer's sinewy legs and touched the skins that adorned the marvelous costume; but Charles Le Mange brushed the impertinent child aside with great dignity, and went to one end of the atrium where a group of women and children were huddled together on the floor, trying to warm themselves as best they could at the small flames from the hearth, which they fed with resinous branches.

Suddenly my excellent personage broke the spell of his own enchantment. Before my wondering eyes, the man tore off the artificial sorrel-colored hair and was transformed into an old man, his weary face covered with deep wrinkles. The slackness of old age shown in his mouth; his eyes alone remained lively and brilliant. A woman helped remove his ostentatious garments, leaving him dressed only in shorts and a cotton shirt; another woman near him solicitously draped a heavy wool poncho over the old man's shoulders. Next to me, two drunken Indians who were watching every detail of the scene remarked:

"Now Charles Le Mange's really over 'n' done with..."

"Yep. Now he's turned back into my old good-for-nothing buddy, Tanilo Santos..."

Meanwhile Tanilo Santos was trying to warm himself at the fire, and he allowed himself to be scrutinized by the people around him.

The January night had fallen; the stars in the wintery sky of Chalma sparkled like the tiny mirrors and spangles adorning the caps and robes of the *Twelve Peers of France*.

"At night, there's nothing more inviting than a fire..." At least, I used that sentiment to approach the circle of Indians assembled around Tanilo Santos.

"There is nothing better for friendship and cheer than a good drink of mescal..." At least, with that opinion I offered the bottle to Tanilo Santos, who accepted the invitation silently, then passed it to the old women surrounding him; they all lifted the bottle to their lips. When Tanilo Santos was certain that everyone had taken a drink, he wiped the mouth of the bottle with his hand and returned it to me without a word... At that moment I was sure that Tanilo Santos had taken the bait, and that he was entirely in my hands.

Stealthily, I separated myself from the group and walked to the courtyard railing, overlooking the river. The torrent roared at my feet, the fierce waters took the curve, embracing the temple that seemed stuck to a large rock; on the other bank, the tree-filled hill, and over it a veil of peace... There I waited, confident that my stratagem would have its effect.

Long minutes went by without the reaction I was hoping for... If unsuccessful, I would have to concoct another scheme to gain the confidence of this Tanilo Santos. I wanted to talk to him to get information for my projected study about the highland Indians' concept of the divinity... I believed that in Tanilo Santos I had found a figure midway between patriarch and big shot, between authority figure and magician, with absolute authority over his people, and for that reason a magnificent informant.

I had nearly given up on the idea of succeeding to engage the old Mazahua in conversation with my first attempt when I saw him stand and wrap himself in his poncho. Then, with a show of great indifference, he set out walking until he came to the railing, but at a good distance from me. There he leaned on his arms and gazed at the stars for a long while, then shifted his eyes to the darkness where the river was holding forth, and finally he threw a stone into the shadows. I watched him covertly, pretending not to notice; I knew that sooner or later Tanilo Santos would feel an urge to renew his friendly relationship with... the bottle of raw whiskey. But now he was at my side; between his fingers the light of a firefly was throbbing. The man graciously held out the insect to me and said:

"Put it in your hat, sir."

I did as he asked, but when the insect found itself free, it took flight. There it went, across the river, a small, furtive star in an even line.

Tanilo Santos laughed happily; flushed with victory, I awaited his request.

"Will your honor be staying for the group from Xochimilco?"

"Yes, I want to hear them sing their version of *Mañanitas al Señor*..."

"They'll be here at daybreak..."

"'Twilight and daybreak, one and the same...' Besides, the night is beautiful."

Tanilo Santos rolled a cigarette from a leaf and sheltered it with his hands to light it, sucking noisily and energetically.

"What do they say in Atlacomulco, Tanilo Santos?" I asked.

"Hmmm... well, the usual," replied the old man rather distrustfully. Then, reverting to his acerbity, he turned to the river, spat thickly, and leaned against the stone railing, completely ignoring me.

I thought the moment had come to use heroic measures; from the hip pocket of my trousers I took out the bottle of whiskey. I held it in front of my eyes, shook it, pulled out the cork and smelled it. I made an elaborate show of pleasure; I took a sip, I smacked my tongue... All these movements were followed by the eyes of Tanilo Santos; he was like a hungry dog waiting for a bite of food. Suddenly he spoke:

"And what do they say in Mexico City, dear *patrón*?"

"Well, the usual," I replied drily, as I stuck the bottle back into my pocket. Without another word, I turned toward the river.

Tanilo was left at a loss, which confirmed my opinion that things were going just as I wanted them to.

"Because back there, in Atlacomulco things aren't so good, you know..." Tanilo continued. "That's the reason we brought our group, by the way. The fact is, Don Donato Becerra has gotten pretty sick, and nothing short of a miracle from the Saint of Chalma is going to be able to save him... That's why we all got together here; to ask him to help us out... It's getting a little chilly, don't you think?"

"A little," I answered.

I felt that this was the right time to release Tanilo Santos from his torture, and to stimulate his tongue at the same time. I held out the bottle to him, he drank delicately. After he wiped his lips with the back of his hand, he gave the bottle back. I had scarcely taken it when the Indian turned his back to me and withdrew into his shell of silence.

I waited calmly for another hint, or for him to ask openly for another drink; but this didn't come as soon as I would have liked.

A woman's voice called to Tanilo Santos; he grunted a mono-syllable, and stood motionless, leaning against the railing. There was another complaint from the women, and he answered in such rude and absolute terms that the meaning was obvious from a distance even if, as in my case, the onomatopoeic Mazahuan language was completely unknown. From within the circle of people there came muttering and the cries of a child; but Tanilo Santos was unmoved.

Between the two of us silence reigned, as if my scheming enticements with the unalloyed design of striking up a friendship with Tanilo Santos—who was growing more and more untractable as time went by—had become completely useless. Now he was bent over, hunched into a tight ball in his colored poncho; occasionally he coughed. A moment came when I thought the Indian had forgotten me; then, to remind him of my presence, I sat on the railing; I swung my feet and began to whistle: *Nana Amalia*. Suddenly, when I thought all was lost, Tanilo Santos turned to me:

"Those old women! Doesn't your honor know of some good remedy for what makes the blood boil? I think my bile has spilled out…"

"Man," I answered happily, "for every malady, there's mescal."

I handed him the bottle again. I realized that this time I would have to be more cajoling with Tanilo Santos, and when he had guzzled down a drink, I insisted on him taking another, and he did not rebuff this invitation, nor the one that followed it. Tanilo Santos attempted to retreat back into his shell, but his euphoria got the better of him.

"The Lord of Chalma won't deny us this miracle…. We spent more than two hundred *pesos* on the journey and preparing the dance… You see! We all know that even though this Lord can work miracles like nobody's business, these days he costs a packet… But I think we paid plenty for the service we want from him. Don't you agree?"

"Easily," I replied. "Did you tell me that you came here to pray for the health of a neighbor?"

"It's for the health of Don Donatito Becerra… All the Mazahuas from Atlacomulco have come to the Sanctuary for that very reason. Look here, your honor, to tell the truth, there's millions of us," and he pointed to the small groups of men scattered throughout the court-yard of Chalma; some asleep, others in priestly positions, seated, silent, wrapped in their serapes, all looking the same: large spots with apparently nothing underneath, fragments of Grecian frets or dark friezes, surrounding the luring spectacle of the flames.

"So everyone really likes Don Donatito Becerra?" I asked.

"It would be good if he recovers," answered the Indian after he had mulled over his reply for a while, then he added: "I hope this little god of Chalma doesn't play tricks...!"

"Is Donato Becerra a friend of the Mazahuas?" I asked again.

"What do you wanna know for? Don't be so curious! I'll tell you, and you'll probably end up taking the whole mess back to Atlacomulco."

"No, I'm not that interested in your affairs. Have another drink, Tanilo Santos?"

"Well, since you're sharing with us, I'll take another; we have to keep our stomachs warm till daybreak... Or what do you think?"

And Tanilo Santos' tongue loosened up again.

"Two months ago Don Donatito attacked the Mazahua lands of Gracias a Dios, he carried off all the little pigs and heifers, and he punched out our ol' fren' Cleto Torres... And when we all went together to the Council Hall to complain, Don Donatito said no and he said no... that they was nothing but Indian tricks. Just think!... That they just wandered into his slaughter house... And the hides of the cattle that had just been cut up had the brand of my ol' fren' Cleto Torres... But that skunk Don Donatito said no and he said no, and he pulled in so much over here and shoveled so much over there, that he ended up planting me and my fren' Cleto Torres in the jail house."

"But is all that really true, Tanilo Santos?"

"Hmm, I wouldn't go telling no lies up so close to the Lord of Chalma... But that's nothin'. The next year what that worthless no-good done was to get it into his head to be a delegate; then he'd do anything for all of us Mazahuas. It was Tanilo Santos this, and Tanilo Santos that... And me, like a fool, I got him a lot of people... Millions, is more like it! You should have seen the square in Atlacomulco, all full of donkeys and Christians... All kinds of pulque, good barbecues, plenty of tortillas made from Indian corn. Trucks and carts out to the towns to carry the Indians; they got us good and drunk, they give us plenty to drink until we were all feeling real good, nobody can deny that... But that was it, all of a sudden another candidate comes out and they call him the PRI; not a soul in the whole place knows him... But anyways, Don Donatito lost his head. Then you should o' seen what happened: Don Donatito, fire coming out of his ears—you should o' seen it! He sent us away, in a rampage, all of us together. We hightailed it on foot back to our little shacks... Just over there in Cerrito Quemado we were caught in a cloudburst that you wouldn't believe... And ever since then Don Donatito doesn't even give a thought to us dumb Indians, unless it's to get the whole flock sheared... He says the Revolution this and the Revolution that, and the national proletariat and stuff about Sinarquism, and while he's making all this ruckus, the only thing he knows how to do is put the screws to us wherever he can... There's what happened in Tlacotepé... Don Donatito got his hands on the Endhó ranch, he threw out the Indians jus' to make farmers out of the rich people in town... Of course, he took the best herdsmen for himself, to the tune that he's a friend of the poor, of those same poor people who go out begging today in the marketplace of Tlacotepé, on account of what Don Donatito did...

"But what happened to the folks in Orocutín was even worse... Don Donatito lost his head over a good-looking little turtledove, but she wouldn't give the old man the time o' day, like they say... Well, there you have it, one night he showed up at the Maguey Blanco ranch where the little bird was sleeping, and carried her off... He left the mother, Jelipa Reyes, all beat up, and he tied up Ruperto Lucas, the father, after he gave him a holy beating... Six months later the turtledove came back to Maguey Blanco with a belly this big... He sent her back on foot, and with nothing more for her stomach than what she was already carrying inside of it...

"Anyway, with his bad ways, Don Donatito Becerra is the richest man in the village... And what was he before? Well, nothing but a pulque-seller at my ol' fren' Matías Lobato's little place."

"But," I asked, "didn't you tell me that Don Donato Becerra is sick?"

"He's sick, real sick... Look, every single one of us Mazahuas got together and made up a plan to finish off Don Donatito (may

God keep him for just a few more months)... As luck would have it, the ones that got him were the Tlacotepés... And the other night, when the fellow was drunk, a poor tramp went up to him and asked him for a few cents. When Don Donatito put his hand in his pocket, all of a sudden three big spots of blood poured out of his back... Nobody knows where the poor little tramp ended up. That Christian has gotten real bad, but none of us—not the people from Atlacomulco, or the ones from Orocutín—want him to die. If he gets better, well, luck gave the people from Orocutín the chance to finish him off... And if Don Donatito stays alive because of the miracle that we all came here to ask the Lord of Chalma for, it will be our turn—the people from Atlacomulco—and then, yes; until his lips are sealed forever... Now, yes, as the saying goes, 'The third time's the charm...'"

"It's so complicated, Tanilo Santos."

"Not really... The Lord of Chalma is expensive, but he comes through!"

Dawn was breaking in Chalma. It was January sixth, Epiphany; coming down the footpath were the people from Xochimilco, a multitude of fragrances, a mass of colors, an echo of praises enveloped them, while rockets flew up until they exploded in the sky, like the glorious schemes of the Mazahuas, of the Tarascans, of the Otomís, of the Pames, of the Matlazincas...

# Our Lady of Nequeteje ⌒

The psychoanalyst's test got everyone's attention. She had brought an album along on the expedition: reproductions of masterpieces of art. There, for example, was the robust and dynamic *Lavinia* of Titian; David's *Napoleon*, a horseman on a silver colt, a penetrating gaze, his index finger held out; Leonardo da Vinci's *Mona Lisa*, smiling at her secret; *Isabel de Valois*, whom Pantoja de la Cruz crowned with prestige and royalty both in mien and in jewelry; *Man* as seen by El Greco; the *Sobbing* by Siqueiros, where woman captures pain in a chilling pose; the pathetic *Tata Jesucristo* of Goitia; the *Zapata* of Diego, saintly-looking, with a large mustache, a spokesman for the hungry and standard-bearer of white causes, like the white pants and white smiles of the Indians; the Trinchera, a crossroads of tragedy and a hotbed of curses, in which José Clemente Orozco's inspiration found form, a protest painted in colors, and so forth...

The natives of that tiny place—Nequetejé—of that miserable hamlet lost in the folds of the Sierra Madre, looked again and again, silently admiring the plates that awakened in them, against the blight of their abuses and the dross of their misgivings, thoughts of royalty and obscure ideals. Eyes boring into lithographs, pupils wide in astonishment, at shades of color, tones and shapes reflecting the same passion, the same fury that the esthetic impact had wrought on their hearts more than on their minds…

In the wake of amazement, there came a new reaction, one that was neither consternation or wonder, but stupor—sacred, silent, disconcerting.

When the psychoanalyst brought her subjects out of their reverie with questions intended to clarify the enigmas, the Indians were uncommunicative: two or three monosyllables dragged out with effort, that seemed to indicate a preference for form over color, which—in their evaluation of art—took precedence over composition and meaning, these being less important in their eyes, possibly because of cultural differences or perhaps because of their own aesthetics. But there could be no doubting the interest those wondrous dabs of paint aroused in these primitives, as they are called by anthropologists, backward, according to ethnological thought, or prelogical, in the opinion of our genteel research associate, the Freudian psychoanalyst.

It was a sight to behold: parents bringing their children in groups, old people coming, with trembling steps, to the little rural schoolhouse where we had set up our laboratory, how they all leaned over the desk where the album lay, how each image was received with a concordant noisy reaction, and how it awakened unconcealable waves of emotion. There was one plate in particular that brought unanimous admiration:

"She is the prettiest…" "The most elegant," were the words heard when it was held up to fascinated eyes.

"No one prettier," said soft, timid voices… And the Mona Lisa intensified her absurd expression as a smiling sphinx, eloquently enigmatic, brilliantly obscure. "She's the most beautiful."

At this clear tendency, the psychoanalyst stopped and revealed the emotion of the Indians to our astonished eyes. It was when she, just like Mona Lisa, smiled, but hers was an innocuous, transparent smile, a triumphant smile, because, according to her findings and her expertise, she had found the key to the collective complex.

One day, back in Mexico City, I visited the psychoanalyst. I sincerely wanted to know her conclusions about the painting test.

She was bright and optimistic because the test was irrefutable: the Pame Indians admired form and appreciated color, while at the same time they thought little of the merits of composition, and perhaps ignored the depths of the creative concept...

But there was something that clearly marked a curious incongruity, a peculiarity that did not fit the statistics, that was impossible to transform into numbers and cram into the austere columns they formed in charts and reports; it was something that escaped methodology, that evaded science the way a thought escapes detection, or a fragrance disappears from the eye of a camera. It was the wonder, the self-abnegation that the Mona Lisa produced in the hearts of the Pames.

"It's really strange, because it doesn't have the brightest colors or the most attractive form. What may have impressed them most about Leonardo's work is its balance, its serenity...," I ventured.

The psychoanalyst smiled at my empirical appraisal. There was an air of pity in her attitude, an expression of sardonic forbearance, that silenced me. Then, to my bewilderment, she launched her theory:

"It happens, my friend, to be a collective neurotic state... a well-defined stage in biogenetics. Yes," she reaffirmed, "the primitive, his soul cloaked in mystery, holds out thrilling surprises for us... His thought is mystifying to everyone because it is contradictory. The primitive, like a child, suffers in enjoyment, loves while he hates, and moans when he laughs. Our Indians from Nequetejé could not escape the laws of psychology. Our contemporary barbaric man is a beehive of complexes. He reasons by simple analysis because he lacks the ability to synthesize—the mark of advanced cultures. In this case they have become bewitched—there's no other word for it—by the painting of the Mona Lisa. They have seen themselves in it; it's as though the entire village stood, one at a time, in front of a mirror. Isn't there, in the undefined, indecisive expression of Mona Lisa a breath of the arcanum similar to that which plays in the smile of the Indian, or an expression that precedes a child's cry. Don't you see in Mona Lisa's face the serenity so marked in the features of the Indians? Doesn't her yellowish skin remind you of the skin-color of our Indians? Isn't her coiffure like that of the little women in Nequetejé? Aren't the robes that adorn this marvelous creation similar to the dress clothes the Indian women wear on feast days? Doesn't the landscape in the background—rugged, rocky land—remind you of the desert setting of the mountains of the Pame?"

"That's true," I answered, a bit disconcerted, "I think that's all very remarkable, but…"

"Look for yourself, let's find the picture and you'll see that it's exactly as I've said."

And the woman's delicate, manicured fingers began to leaf through the album, searching for the Mona Lisa. The entire collection of prints passed before our eyes once, then twice, but the one we were looking for never appeared.

The young professional fixed her surprised eyes on mine, and at the same time she said enthusiastically:

"It's gone…! They stole it, don't you see!"

"But are you sure it was the Indians?"

"Yes, absolutely certain; no one has touched the album except me since we came back from Nequetejé. I didn't even look through it myself after the last experiment… It was them, there's no doubt in my mind… Look, they had to take the screws out so they wouldn't tear the plate… Oh yes, this one is missing a little screw; they probably didn't have time to put it back in…"

"It's too bad they've taken part of such a valuable test," I said stupidly.

"What they've done is absolutely eloquent, and I'd give a dozen albums like this one to have gotten it… Don't you see that the theft fully corroborates my conclusion about collective psychology?"

Then, ignoring me, she opened a notebook and became lost in a sea of notations.

A year later I had to make some corrections and verify certain vague reports in order to publish the fruits of our research; so I went back to Nequetejé. This time I was given lodging in the chapel sacristy. There, an uncomfortable, dirty and cold room was made up for me. The chaplain, who had arrived only recently himself, was an amiable and hospitable old fellow that I made friends with immediately. He informed me that the Pames in that area hadn't had a parish for twenty-five years, and that he had taken on the task of reorganizing the church and its services.

"How sad it must be, sir, to live in such a desolate, out of the way place," I told him.

"My friend," he replied, "when the flock is large and easily frightened, the shepherd doesn't look at the landscape."

I went out to the miserable village's little plaza for a few moments, beneath the shade of the ash trees, to enjoy the cool air. My presence soon caused a stir among the people. An old woman came up to me and whined:

"We all know what you're here for. Watch out…"

And without another word, she continued on her way, step by step. Her bare, hesitant feet made furrows instead of prints in the sandy ground.

Then it was a surly adult male who approached me, a farmer's machete hanging from his left shoulder.

"If you take what you came for, you'll pay with your hide," he said in a hoarse, stumbling voice.

"But, what are you talking about?" I asked.

"That's all I'm going to say… If you won't take no for an answer, you won't get out of Nequetejé alive," he added in a determined tone.

Then he spat thickly and left.

Immediately, grisly little groups of three or four men hemmed me in. In the doorways of their huts, women watched me with disturbing eyes. I went over to one of them, and before her insistent stare, I asked her:

"Why is everyone looking at me?"

"Jus' to have a look, and see when you're going to die, you sneak thief," she replied with a smile as sharp as the needle of a maguey.

Twilight erupted in a commotion of chirping and caterwauling. The first call for the rosary chimed out. I took advantage of the instant that peace fell with the clamor of the bell, and went to the sacristy. At that moment the chaplain was getting into the worn surplice, and pulling the sweat-stained, tattered stole around his neck, he smiled at me, and remarked:

"In these out of the way places, even ecclesiastical work offers some distraction… Isn't that so, my son?"

I didn't answer. I went to the church. Fragrances of copal and myrrh invaded my nostrils; spirals of smoke from incensories and braziers rose to the vault which covered a multitude of people, prostrate, in an inexpressible demonstration of faith. Half a hundred faithful of all ages united in a common belief, absolute, infectious. The little church was dirt-poor; whitewashed walls, a flooring of porous, sweating bricks, worm-eaten window casings and cracked glass; a narrow chancel, a tarnished altar made of broken plaster, and a damp, black tabernacle. A small, brown, Indian-looking Christ hung from a cross, covered in roses made of discolored paper. The rest of the church was bare, cold, wretched... except for one picture attached to the transept on the right. There, a solemn, flickering flame was born from altar candles and tapers: the little altar adorned with a pure white tablecloth, richly embroidered; multicolored spheres, branches of trees, and small wildflowers, and above it, an image with a frame of stout mesquite around it, from which a multitude of silver offerings were hanging...

But, what did my eyes see...! Yes, it was she, our Mona Lisa, the picture stolen from the psychoanalyst's test. Yes, there could be no doubt, there she was, deified, bestowing favors on her flock, as demonstrated by the silvery miracle stories that hung from the broad picture-frame, and by the fervor of the people, prostrate at her feet.

The faithful had turned their backs on the Indian Christ to face the Florentine image, to which mystical theology had become attached with incredible force. I contemplated this feat for a few brief seconds, but quickly realized the risk I was running when that small crowd would notice my presence and think I had come to take back the lithograph they had stolen, and carry it away with me. I turned, and went back into the sacristy. When the chaplain saw my agitation, he talked to me about it:

"Yes, my friend, it's all a pagan affair... I know how the lithograph got here as well as you do. When I came to this village I found it already enthroned, and I immediately tried to remove it from the church, but my attempt was frustrated by an opposition that, in the end, became aggressive. They call her Our Lady of Nequetejé, and they swear she is more miraculous than any patronage of the Holy Virgin. Her cult has spread to the natives for miles around, and they come to see her in processions, in huge, fervent pilgrimages. They sing praises to her before her altar, and they perform quaint dances in her honor. They feel a blind devotion to this lithograph, and it would be very difficult to tear it from their hearts. There would also be a danger that the attempt would do harm to a generalized—and therefore respectable—sentiment. Now then, being weak, I sidestep the problem, and I ready myself to channel that faith toward truth, one day, when the Lord permits me... In the meantime, I leave them to their innocent error. If I am doing wrong, may God forgive me!"

Inside the chapel a chorus of praises had burst out for the virgin, pure and immaculate. Mona Lisa, the impudent, jovial wife of Zenobi il Giocondo, smiled at this new adventure, the most prodigious of her history, more sublime than that in which the Genius da Vinci illuminated her with immortal lights, more extraordinary than her reported abduction from the Louvre Museum... Now, in Nequeteje, she was working miracles, and they were attributing to her, along with virginity, the motherhood of God.

In the laboratory, in Mexico City, the researcher claimed to have extracted, in a simple cipher, in a number many times smaller than the whole, the entire essence of this incident, in order to illustrate a scientific conclusion that would reveal to her countrymen and to foreigners, the soul of the Indians in Mexico.

Meanwhile, in distant Nequeteje, long candles of devotion and oil lamps burn, nourished with the essence of hope.

# The Goat on Two Hooves ⌒

At a bend in the road where the air becomes a whirlwind, Juá Shotá, the Otomí Indian, set down his roots. In the rocky mountains, where the sun strikes, the vagabond came to a halt. A boulder shaded his body, while the valley offered tranquility and delight to his eyes. Around him grew stalks of corn, barely two hands-breadth in height, that were withering away, weak and sickly. The Indian was an undismayed witness to the sweat and tears that had been spilled upon the planting to quench the thirst of the sown fields and the hunger of the sowers.

Juá Shotá passed his days at a vegetable-like rhythm, clinging to the rock, blending in, like the trees from Peru, living like the agave, atop its calcareous mantle.

To the traveler he would offer a gourd-cup of *pulque* at the very instant when the legs grew weak and the tongue stuck to the palate. The reward for this service was modest, but so constant that one day a shelter burst forth from the large rock: and it was an oasis in the desert, the cream of this region. A shelter that offered everything to the traveler, who never passed up the satisfaction of sitting in its shade for a brief spell.

When a framework of timbers appeared at the rear of the hut, tied together with tips of lettuce fiber, its nooks covered with bottles that bore colored labels: lemonade, *"ferroquina,"* raspberry, or with packs of cigarettes made of very strong tobacco, or with tins of hard crackers, or with leather straps, or *ayate*-bags—these being indispensable items in taverns where they were much in demand by the clientele of porters and peddlers,—then María Petra arrived, obedient to the summons of Juá Shotá, her husband.

Like a mushroom, the woman sprouted one afternoon between the boulders. She arrived exhausted; locks of black hair fell over her forehead; sweat from her body soaked the shirting that covered her; she put her hardened feet down, one after another, searching for rest. Bent by the weight of the burden wrapped in an *ayate*-bag, her breasts swayed like bells. The traveler's hands were not empty; in them a spindle moved, twisting, continually twisting, as it was caressed by thumb and index finger, a line, a thread of *ixtle*-fiber, the warp and woof of the Indian life.

Juá Shotá came out to meet her, and his words welcomed her. Then he asked about something he could not see. With a grimace she set down her burden, and from the mass, she lifted a bundle—out of which sprang a child's cries. Then Juá Shotá caressed his bedraggled, ugly daughter, María Agrícola.

The mother, not daring to look, smiled.

The narrow stretch, where the trail led, widened slowly as the years passed by, one by one. Juá Shotá's inn had grown, and it had earned a reputation: Any traveler passing along that uninviting path was a traveler who stopped to go inside the wretched shop and whet his whistle with a swallow of raw whiskey or to refresh himself with a small jug of *pulque*. By now, Juá Shotá was a fat man, garrulous in manners and speech. He dressed in the whitest of clothing, and wore cowhide *huarache*-sandals on his feet. To keep up with his new status, he had changed his surname, and now his clientele knew him as Don Juan Nopal. María Petra, on the other hand, slaved away at her hard labor indoors, in her never-ending struggle with the stony trumpery of household objects.

The girl grew up among crags and gorges. Her copper-colored skin shown through the tattered clothing she wore; her flat-nosed face framed her fawn-like eyes, and her supple body combined graceful lines with dark curves.

María Agrícola lived in isolation from the world. Don Juan Nopal and María Petra, he absorbed in running the inn, and she devoted to the care of the home, neglected the spirited young girl who spent the entire day in the countryside. There, she ran from rock to rock as she took the herd to its watering-hole. She ate prickly pears and mesquite; she quarreled with the wolf, frightened the small tiger and disdainfully threw stones at the shepherd, her neighbor, who, with suspect intentions, tried more than once to block her path. When day was done she rounded up the herd, and humming a little tune, she followed her flock and left them locked up in the craggy corral, not forgetting first to ward off harmful animals with solemn, mysterious words. Then she went back to her house, ate a good share of *tortillas* with chile, drank a jug of pulque and lay down on the palm-mat, caught in the clutches of sleep.

Don Juan Nopal's clientele grew steadily. Travelers paraded through the inn: mule-drivers from the mountains, lively, boasting half-breeds who came to the doors of the hut while outside their sweaty, lank mules stood laboring under the load of sugar, of whiskey, or of semitropical fruits. These benefactors chatted and cursed loudly, they gorged themselves with food and drank alcoholic beverages like they were water. When it came time to pay, they outdid themselves.

Or the Indians who carried the product of an entire week's work on their backs: two dozen pots made of baked clay, destined for the nearest marketplace. These traders occupied the farthest corner of the tavern. There they waited quietly for the gourd-cup of pulque, and drank it in silence. They paid for what they consumed with copper-coins, slippery from being counted so often, and then quickly went off with their eternal little trot.

Or the Otomís who, in order to carry out a penance, walked league after league bearing an image on a litter escorted by ten or twelve companions. Each of them hauled along a string of children, behind the ass loaded down with two wineskins full of *pulque* that grew continually lighter with the assaults of the thirsty ones. Then fireworks exploded against the sky, the women were wailing, filled with piety, and the men alternated shouts of praise with highly

irreverent songs, accompanied by a six-string guitar and a hand or-
gan engaged in melodic combat. Once they reached Juan Nopal's
place they forgot the pulque and laid into the raw-whiskey. In no
time at all the place was about to burst; the men celebrated the rak-
ish tall-tale and the scatological incident with boisterous laughter, or
they engaged in rough hand-games. The women pressed together
tightly, and with their vision clouded by flowing tears they continued to drink with the same fervor as when they offered up supplica-
tions and prayers. The saint on the litter lay in neglect in the middle
of the room.

Or the caravan that accompanied a cadaver, three days dead,
carried on the backs of family members who took turns and periodi-
cally spelled each other. A cadaver that had climbed mountains,
crossed valleys, forded rivers, and wandered in the blackness of abysses,
eager to cut the distance between the little town lost in the moun-
tain-range and the capital of the municipality where the most pro-
ductive resource was a prerogative to have cemeteries. This wailing
throng reached Don Juan Nopal's house, and after repeated libations
to the health of the dear faithful departed, they cleaned out the wine-
cellar, while the corpse, stretched out in the middle of the road, thundered out gruesomely.

With this clientele, Juan Nopal made a living. Peace encom-
passed the roof of this home in the mountain. The view was poor,
blocked by the side of a hill that rose up between the lands of the
Otomí and the broad valley.

When that married couple set up their camp tent across from
Juan Nopal's tavern, he felt, without knowing why, a great sympathy
for the new arrivals. The man's color was pale, he had a large stomach, and his mannerisms were somewhat affected. He wore glasses of
the type that make the Indian laugh out loud whenever he sees them
portrayed in the newspapers that occasionally fall into his hands.

Every morning the new neighbor went out, looking with every
step he took for stones that he then brought back to his tent. In the
afternoons he ground down the rough rocks and carefully examined
the dust.

She was a delicate, timid young woman. Her physique did not
suit her apparel: trousers made of coarse cloth that made her gluteus

maximus stand out grotesquely, to the glee of Nopal and his clientele; boots made of oiled leather, and a straw hat that she fastened around her neck with a red ribbon. Nonetheless, when the owner of the tavern saw how mountain life created problems for the delicate woman, he felt some inexplicable compassion for her.

The man seemed more accustomed to the hardships of rustic life; he came and went with unvarying steps. At times he sang something in a hoarse, powerful voice that sounded very comical to Juan Nopal.

The foreigner's activities had the Indian intrigued. The muleteers who traveled the mountains said that from his boots, his wide, bell-bottom pants and his chimney-pot hat, they could see clearly that the neighbor was an engineer. From that day on, Don Juan Nopal referred to the man in the camping tent as the engineer.

One afternoon María Agrícola came back, breathless.

"Hey, Poppa," she said to her father in their language, "that one, the one you call an engineer, he followed me all around the mountain."

"He probably wanted you to help him pick up those big rocks of his that he goes out looking for every day..."

"Big rocks? No, he was acting like a goat, Father... I wanted to muzzle him down under an acacia tree and throw a jug of cold water on his back..."

The eyes of the Indian became veiled.

The engineer came to the inn. He asked for a glass of lemonade, and began to drink it slowly. He talked about many things. He said that he was a miner, and that he had come to the mountain range, looking for silver. That his wife had come along simply to do chores for him... That he was rich and powerful.

The Indian only listened: "Since he talks much, he wants much," he mused to himself, repeating the maxim his parents had taught him. "But one who talks much gets little," he added as a small postscript of his own.

When María Agrícola passed by in front of them, the Indian saw how the engineer grew perturbed, and noticed the unmistakable glint in his eyes.

The next day the man repeated his visit, except this time his

wife was with him. Don Juan Nopal was captivated by the gentleness of the woman's manners, as well as the sadness deep in her green
eyes. Her quiet voice caressed the innkeeper's ear, at the same time
that her long, fine hands lay hold of his heart. That afternoon he was
pleased by the miner's visit.

The engineer's visits to the store became more frequent. He
drank lemonade while he said strange things that the Indian could
scarcely fathom… But he laughed and laughed anyway, because he
found the talk so comical.

"All right, Don Juan," the miner finally said, "I have a good
business deal for you."

"Tell me about it, sir," answered the Otomí.

"Are the cattle very expensive around here? How much, for
example, would a little she-goat end up costing?"

"Around here no one sells cattle. The few animals we got, we
keep 'em for when it's our turn to be the stewards of Saint Nicholas,
the one us people from Bojay pray to—that's my land—over there
on the other side of the tallest hill you can see behind the branches of
that *pirul*-tree… Or for the day the Holy Child of the Port comes
a'visiting us. Then we have them butchered, and we don't even spare
the milking-goats, because lots of people come."

"All right, all right, but if I offer you ten pesos for a little she-
goat, would you be willing to sell her to me?"

"Well, prob'ly not even then," answered the Indian, feigning
little desire to bargain.

"Ten big *pesos*, man; nobody will give you more… Because what
I'm willing to pay for is really just a whim of mine."

Don Juan didn't answer, but he put on an expression that was
so ambivalent, anyone would have thought he was accepting.

"In among your livestock, Don Juan, there's a she-goat that I
like a lot—so much that you can see what kind of money I'm willing
to pay you for her."

"If you want her, sir, you'll have to pay me in copper pennies
and five-cent pieces… We ain't got no liking for paper money."

"You'll have the ten *pesos* in copper, you suspicious old man."

"If you've already had a look at the little animal, sir, go to the
mountain and get it."

"It's just," said the miner brassily, "that the she-goat I want has two hooves."

"Ha, ha, ha," the Indian laughed loudly. "And I didn't want to believe the mountain mule-drivers, but now I'm sure of it; you're crazy, sir... you're plumb crazy! She-goats with two hooves. It would have to be the wife of Old Nick, you!"

"A she-goat with two hooves is what I'm calling your daughter... Don't you understand, you idiot?" the stranger asked irritably.

The Indian dropped the smile that had been hanging on his lips after the laughter, and fixed an eye on the miner, trying to penetrate into the abyss of that proposition.

"Say something, blink if nothing else, you heathen," the white man shouted angrily. "Decide, once and for all. Are you going to sell me your daughter? Yes or no?"

"Doesn't it make you ashamed, sir? It would be as ugly for me to sell her as it would be for you to buy her... Women give themselves to men of their own race, when they're not already promised and when they can drive the plough."

"When a person charges enough and is well paid, there's no shame, Don Juan," said the engineer, softening his tone. "Race has nothing to do with it... and even less when it's a matter of the race that you Indians want to preserve... A fine breed that has no use except to frighten children who go to museums!"

"Well, that sort of she-goat can't be all that ugly, dear sir, since you're so interested in one of them."

"I told you it was just a whim of mine... You'll probably come out of it gaining a little half-breed grandson. A child of a white man who will be more intelligent than you are. A half-breed who will be worth more than ten *pesos* in copper."

"No, that stock is not for sale," replied Don Juan in a tone that indicated he had not understood or had not wanted to understand his client's last words.

"You'd have to be stupid not to deal. On the coast they give away virgin Indian girls, just on the hope that they'll have a white child, because those people understand that the blending of men is as useful as good interbreeding is in cattle; but you Otomís are so closed-minded that you won't give in to bettering yourselves even if you get paid for it."

Now there was a flame in Don Juan's eyes. A flame that the

white man, in the heat of his temper, did not notice.

"All right, in view of your foolishness, I'll double the offer. Twenty *pesos* for her. Twenty *pesos* in copper coins worth five each! No, I won't take her away with me, because Indian servants in the city are worthless sows. I just want you to tell her to bathe, and advise her not to act badly with me; tell her not to scratch me or kick me... Afterward I'll leave her with you. I'm just paying for your silence, because I wouldn't want anyone to find out about it, you know?" he said as he glanced back at the camp tent where the white woman sat mending clothes, near the door.

"No sir, you are a bad person. I already told you, I'm not that kind... And besides, you don't pay enough!"

"Twenty-five *pesos*, in copper... In copper, you heard me," the buyer offered conclusively.

"I'm going to teach you, sir, how to trade in cattle," the Otomí said phlegmatically as he took a heavy bag out of the money drawer at the counter. "There are one-hundred *pesos* here, in copper... And since I believe, the same way you do, that crossbreeding is good, I'd like to better my bloodline too. But my own, not somebody else's. I'll give you a hundred *pesos* for your wife. Just bring her to me, I won't put any conditions on it... Even if she scratches me, bites me, or up and kicks me. And I won't pay you to keep quiet about it, I'll give you that for nothin'. You can tell the whole world. You don't have to wash her either; just give her to me the way she is."

Now it was the engineer's turn to be silent.

"Then you take her away with you, sir; she won't do me no good here on the mountain... She might even break to pieces! She's your burden, sir. But this you can be assured of: You have my guarantee that soon you'll have a pretty, hardworking half-breed who'll call you Papa... Interbreedings are good; but the best part about them is that it can go from male to female the same way it can from female to male... Or what's your opinion, sir?"

"But that's beastly... You're letting your tongue get away with you, you savage."

"You decide then," continued Juan, "because when I'm excited, I get a little scatterbrained. A hundred *pesos*, in copper. No one will give you more, since she's so puny. Why, with her weight she can hardly make the scale go up. I'm not buying her flesh or her hide, I'll only buy a certain little something about her from you, sir... But if

you don't like this arrangement, I have a different proposal for you...
You decide!"

Both of their gazes fell on one single point. Four eyes were fixed on a machete hanging from the counter within reach of the Indian's hand.

"A hundred *pesos* for a certain little something, Mister Engineer!" repeated Don Juan scornfully. On his lips there was a smile that rivaled the coldness of the steel blade.

The following morning Don Juan Nopal was surprised not to find the engineer's camp tent across from his house. It had been taken down hastily, before midnight. Dawn had overtaken the white fugitives on the top of El Jilote hill.

María Agrícola, stretching her fine, supple body, like an archer's instrument, let the breeze stir the blackness of her tresses, as she watched how a cloud of dust rose off in the distance, near the ravine of El Cántaro, a point adjoining the railroad tracks.

# THE TEN RESPONSORIES ⟨

It was Monday afternoon. He lay on the shoulder of the highway, arms outstretched in the shape of a cross. On his coppery dust-covered face an expression of surprise lingered, and his half-open eyes were horribly cross-eyed, showing very plainly his final convulsion. Near him, the ass, loaded down with two bundles of firewood and an inflated skin of pulque; closer still, Tlachique, the tailless, bony dog, was scratching his mange, while making certain to keep his master's body in sight.

This is how the people, returning from the farmer's market in Ixmiquilpan to the town of Panales, found the body of Plácido Santiago. Panales, cowering in humility at the edge of the highway that travels from Mexico City to Laredo.

Some of the men were drunk as they walked along. The lowly women went in front of the procession, loaded down with their purchases or with the products of their labors that had not been sold in the local market.

The discovery caused general consternation. A group pressed near the lifeless body of their countryman, Plácido Santiago.

"It was an automobile."

"I'm a thinkin' it was a truck."

"Damn them, ever since they opened up the road to these devils a body ain't safe outside no more, not even on their own lands."

An old woman knelt next to the body; she moistened her thumb and first finger with saliva, and rubbed them over the yellowish earlobes of Plácido Santiago. From the old woman's mouth sprang a prayer that a chorus of grieving voices echoed.

The eldest took the initiative. Two young men helped him unload the ass.

"There will be plenty of wine for the wake," said one with satisfaction, as he held the swollen wineskin in his arms.

"That's so," agreed another as he loaded the wineskin onto his back.

"You, Tomás, get the bundle of wood... It's my Auntie Trenidá's inheritance from Plácido Santiago," said the old man everyone called Uncle Roque.

Then, several men working together sat the body upright on the burro. The legs, open, stiff, hung like calipers on the beast's belly; the toes, sticking out of *huarache*-sandals, were like yellowed bunches of grapes, like fruit spoiled by frost; the mop of hair on his enormously broad head stirred at the breath of chilly December air.

Behind the ass came men and women, walking slowly, solemnly. From time to time the animal nipped at the shoots of dog's grass, giving no heed to the lashing that followed his greedy attempts... But during one of these, the body came close to rolling off. There was a cry of alarm, and shouts. Roque Higuera, the Uncle, had a boy climb onto the croup of the ass and hold the remains of Plácido Santiago in place.

The caravan continued on its way until it lurched onto the trail to Panales. In the rear guard, Tlachique, with a watchful eye, his tongue hanging out, panted from the wolf-like little trot he had taken up.

Auntie Trenidá took in the body of her husband, Plácido Santiago, without tears. The pain that had caught in her throat, her heart paralyzed by such a heavy weight, kept her from talking. She swept the dirt-floor of the hut with some acacia branches, then went looking for a bottle of holy-water and sprinkled it on the four walls. Afterward she crushed some lumps of lime in a grinding stone and with the powder she drew a large, wide cross in the middle of the floor. Upon it, with the help of the neighbors, she placed the cadaver that persisted in maintaining the absurd spread-eagle position that the belly of the ass had forced upon its legs. But this irregularity needed to be corrected because it wasn't right to have a cadaver in this position. There was a good strap of rawhide leather lying there. With it, Auntie Trenidá tied the very skinny feet of Plácido Santiago, and she pulled and pulled until they were in the proper position. After laying a medallion of the Virgin de la Merced on the dead man's chest, Auntie Trenidá sat on her heels very close to him. Over her face she had placed a veil and had become quite still, like the silhouette of a frieze.

But now the mourners were arriving. One of them poked a tallow candle as thin as a person's little finger into the ground; another spread yellow funeral flowers on the pavement; one woman left a bunch of broom at the dead man's feet. The smell of open fields filled the air. Someone began the prayer that gradually became a noise like that of the river or the wind playing at the rounded edges of linens.

Uncle Roque Higuera informed the group that, using his own money, he had sent someone off to find the priest of Ixmiquilpan so that he would pray ten responsories costing a *tostón*, on behalf of their friend, Plácido Santiago's soul. The people looked with admiration and appreciation at the old man, overindulged on pulque, whose pocket had been made as unsteady as his tongue.

Afternoon came, then evening and late night. The skin of *pulque* had succumbed to the assaults of the mourners. Uncle Roque Higuera, with increasing splendor, sent his own wine jug out to be filled with another ration equal to what they had consumed: "Now on, it's all a' goin' on my account... Don't worry... It's nothing!" he said splendidly.

The mourning began to turn into a party; everyone was talking loudly. In one corner were the eulogizers of the heretofore unrecognized merits of the deceased. In another, the enthusiastic panegyrists of the excellent qualities of ol' Uncle Plácido Santiago, and the accolades loudly proclaimed by the women as well. Suddenly a sharp, wailing cry sprang from the soft murmur. It was Auntie Trenidá, opening the floodgates of her pain.

In a small corner of the hut, coffee was boiling in a large-bellied pot that rested on a hearth made of three stones. Diligent hands stoked the fire with corn cobs and cow dung.

Outside, *nopal* needles split the stars, crickets accompanied the symphony of howling from the mountain: it was wild dogs, dogs without a master, barking at hunger and at death.

Few were still on their feet when dawn broke. The women, wrapped in their shawls, were nodding off. Some men had stretched out on the stone wall, face up, while others were talking loudly about the punishments of purgatory, the tortures of hell where an earthen pan boiled pork rinds of the soul; about the peace of heaven, made pleasant by a divine mariachi band comprised of philharmonic seraphim, and backed up by trumpet-playing angels and harp-strumming cherubim... In the glory that only the souls of the just enjoy: that, "without offending those present," is where Plácido Santiago is, "God rest his soul..."

From time to time Auntie Trenidá left her hieratic position and used her cramped fingers to pull out the blackened wick that made one of the candles smoke more than usual as it was about to go out.

Roosters hailed the dawn. Their bawdy song silenced the sullen canine concert. The sun lined the hills with rays of dawn, the blackbird gave reply to the linnet's good morning, and darkness gradually lifted to give way to a splendid morning.

In the hut, still sleepy voices sang the *Miserere*. A child cried, overcome by smoke from the copal that rose from an earthen pan brimming with hot coals.

Suddenly everyone turned their eyes toward the box made of fresh wood, still dripping sap as it arrived at the hut on the shoulders of four neighbors... Auntie Trenidá wept a little. Then she wrapped her shawl around herself to comfort the grief welling up in her chest.

The group of men, full of circumspection and correctness, lay the body of Plácido Santiago in the coffin. Uncle Roque Higuera called on Auntie Trenidá to say the final farewell to her companion. With trembling fingers the woman took the cold chin speckled with hard, faded whiskers. Then Uncle Roque Higuera drove in twelve nails with a stone.

While this was being done, the priest from Ixmiquilpan appeared at the helm of his old Ford, and drove right up to the door of the hut. Everyone sank to their knees; the priest raised his right hand

and gave his blessing to each of them. Then the women hurried forward to kiss the plump hand that, reluctantly, he held out to them.

"Quickly, quickly," said the priest. "Let's get this over with: I have a baptism in Remedios, and a viaticum in Tamaleras... Quickly, quickly!"

The father sprinkled the coffin, then from the pouch of his cassock he extracted a breviary and began the prayers. After reciting the ten responsories that had been stipulated, he began to bless the cadaver, but the drunken voice of Uncle Roque Higuera cut him short:

"Just a minute, dear Father, I counted the responsories, and they was ten, sure enough... But don't your grace want to throw one more on the dearly departed as a bonus?"

Slightly miffed, the priest protested:

"I told you, I'm in a hurry... Viaticum in Tamaleras, baptism in Remedios..."

"Come on, come on, just remember, for us it don't make no matter if it's you or the father from Alfajayucan, and you know he never has to be begged... He even drinks pulque."

Then the priest hurriedly recited what, a moment before, he had needed a book for: a breviary that, more than a guide, was an element of splendor in the liturgy... Anyway, it was a bonus, free, gratis!

When four boys lifted the bier and began the funeral march, Uncle Roque Higuera put a five-peso bill in the clergyman's hands.

Everyone there set off behind the coffin except Auntie Trenidá who, curled into a ball of insignificance, sat in front of the hearth. Within reach was a pot full of cooked beans, and the woman was eating them by the handful. When the priest happened to see her at such an unheard of task, he cried out, loudly:

"Holy Mary, Mother of God! Anyone would think you didn't care at all that your husband is dead, daughter... How could you be hungry under these circumstances? Woman, your sin is gluttony!"

Auntie Trenidá wiped her mouth with the back of her hand, she finished chewing what was still between her tongue and palate, and said:

"Last night they wouldn't eat my beans because we were drinking pulque... Nobody even tasted them." Then, her eyes full of tears, she continued: "My husband, with the help of your holy responsories, is enjoying the company of God right now... He took my heart to the grave with him, nobody can ever take his place... But that's no reason for me to let the beans go bad."

Without another word, the priest started up the ancient motor of his automobile, he tramped on the clutch..., then shoved it into first, and raised a curtain of dust between himself and the drama.

Auntie Trenidá, tears flowing down her cheeks, stuck her hand in the pot again:

"Of course it's a sin to let them go," she said, "expensive as they are today..."

Resting on his back paws, Tlachique, the tailless, bony dog, waited his turn, while his tongue licked out again and again...

# THE PLAZA OF XOXOCOTLA ❧

"The plaza of Xoxocotla is pretty; it's pretty and it's clean," I said, without intending flattery.

"It has its history, just like our school and the running water," old Eleuterio Ríos informed me as he stroked his untamed mustache with thumb and index finger; that mustache spattered with lines of silver and that, if one believed the refrain that says, "when the Indian turns gray, the Spaniard dies away," would be a bad joke on the youthful appearance and arrogant countenance of my friend, and he would be judged a man in the prime of his life (which would be a lie).

"Yes, it has its history," repeated the old man who had an irrepressible desire to tell it. Without further hesitation, he spun the story in his slow voice, puffing on the rolled cigarette held between his yellowed teeth.

"I was delegate for the town council when the procession arrived, with the candidate at their head. Don't think for a minute that they wanted to come here, no... The fact is, they were on their way to Puente de Ixtla. But right over there, at the curve of El Tordo, one of the tires on their Ford blew out and they had to stop off here, in Xoxocotla, to find some shade and get a drink of water.

"The candidate was real tall, serious and very quiet. His companions were different: they talked a lot but, like parrots, they didn't even understand their own drivel.

"Someone told me they were going to promote the candidate to be President of the Republic. I didn't believe it... Those toadies are so full of tricks! It seemed like the candidate could read my mind because he stood there looking at me with a little smile, more with his eyes than with his mouth. Then he said:

"'What is it this town needs most, Mr. Delegate?'

"I decided I'd have to go along with the game, and just for tomfoolery, I said to him:

"'Well, as your honor can see, this plaza in Xoxocotla is real sad-looking. It's nothing but a great big piece of dirt, and the only decoration it has is that one bare little acacia tree, standin' all by itself, right in the middle there, and it don't even give enough shade for a rooster... The people in this town, we'd like a plaza with sidewalks, lawns, and shops with lights all around...'

"'You'll have it,' said the candidate, his face deadpan serious.

As for me, I almost burst out laughing, God's truth, at the bald-faced way he had of making fun of people. But just to go along with the story, I pretended to be real happy, and I says to him:

"'There's no school here neither. Look, your honor: look at them poor children all crowded together in that little spot of shade from the church towers. Does your honor really think they can learn anything that-a-way? And they don't even have no teacher! Doña Andrea Sierra can understan' reading, and sometimes she gives them a lesson; she comes and takes them once a week...'

"'You'll have a school,' the candidate promised again, so calm and sure that he got me rattled for a second. But when I remembered that it's the job of everybody who goes up for being a candidate to spout nothing but lies, well then, I stood there just a' staring at him, long and hard, the way we do out here when we want to make fun of someone. That man didn't understand, or he pretended not to understand, what I was doing, and then I started in play-acting with him again. The townspeople was all having a real good time, watching how I was pulling the leg of that there politician:

"'Just like you see, we got plenty of water out here, but we don't have no pipes. Since you're coming around, trying to make all us town folk happy, why don't you just find some way to get us a fountain to spout clear water in the middle of the plaza, with evergreens all around it, and *juanitas* and violets... and the girls with their little round, wet jars, and the boys, wiser than their years, watching them out of the corner of their eye, just the way God wants the male to look at a female who sweeps him off his feet... And the little kids in school, and in the school a real elegant and pretty teacher, teaching all of 'em the syllables...'

"Then my dotty friend, Próculo Delgadillo, he couldn't keep from laughing out loud; but the candidate, real serious, said:

"'You'll have your plaza, your school, your fountain and your teacher.' Then he stood up to say good-bye. He held out his hand. I barely touched it, just to show I wasn't brought up with bad manners, but in a way so he would know we weren't all that stupid.

"When they left, all the neighbors gathered around the little acacia tree. The young men thought the candidate's promises was genuine, and they were real happy; but us old ones who've gotten gray and wrinkled from all our waiting for the politicians to make good on what they say, well, we just stood back an' laughed at the inexperience of the youngsters."

Don Eleuterio was silent for a moment. He removed his enormous straw-hat, and from deep inside its crown took out a little box of matches. He struck one, cupping his hands around the flame and lit his large cigarette of brown tobacco, puffing at it heavily. Then he continued his tale:

"A year went by. I was about to hand the office of delegate over to my friend, Remigio Morales—God rest his soul. It was noontime, a real scorcher. The hot sun was blazing down on that desert we call a plaza. The pigs were squealing, thinking they was about to melt. The chickens were scratching at the hot sand with beaks wide open and their wings flung out, trying to find some way to keep cool. The dogs were going around with their tail hanging between their legs, slobbering like they was sick. The women in the kitchens had taken off their blouses, and the little kids were going around stark-naked, looking for any little old spot of shade, and begging for a drink of water.

"The policeman and me was having a whiskey right over there at Trina Laguna's place... Then, suddenly, Tirso Moya—who was just a little shaver back then, about this high—comes in all flustered, and he says to me: 'Come quick, Tata Luterio, the President's looking for you.' Meantime, I downed my little jug of pulque and asked for another one... It was so hot! I drank it slow, still gabbing with the policeman... And then who comes in but Lucrecita, the daughter of my stepson, Gerardo: 'The President's outside, lookin' for you, Tata Luterio...' 'Go on, get out of here,' I said, 'go find me a left-handed shovel.' And the little girl took off runnin', lickety-split... It wasn't half a second later when that half-wit Odilón Pérez showed up, and says to me in that idiot voice of his: 'The Presidunt, he's outside there, a' waiting on you, Tata Luterio...' 'Well, you tell him,' I answered, 'that if he can't hold his britches for just a while longer, then I can't give him the time of day...' And that idiot Odilón went right out to deliver my message just the way I said it.

"'He must have come for last Monday's money for the plaza,' I said to the policeman.

"We kep' right along, having one drink after another, just takin' our own good, sweet time, not in no hurry. Real careful, I counted all the coins that I'd collected for the plaza and kept wrapped up under my belt. I stayed on to listen to a wild, off-color story that the policeman told me, an' then I went outside, chewing on a piece of barbecued meat that Doña Trina Laguna gave me.

"And what do I see...! Who do you suppose it was? Well, the candidate. There he was, in the sliver of shade from the acacia tree. There was more than twenty little kids all around him, and he was laughing with them, and he had the littlest one in his arms. All the women were standing in the doorway of their houses, looking at him and admiring him; but he didn't even notice, he was so wrapped up in the kids... He had come out here all by himself, just like the little acacia tree; his Ford was sitting there, out on the road... It was just from the way he looked that I knew he'd been promoted to President of the Republic... Big and tall, serious and confident, like all those people who've been raised in rich families, I don't know what there was about him that reminded me of Emiliano. They didn't look alike at all, but the way he acted, the way he took to kids... I don't know. Well, they didn't even dress the same way, but this fellow looked as good in his Texas hat as the other one did in his Mexican hat—the way some people say he still appears to them today when they take the road to Chinameca.

"Feeling real ashamed, I went up to him. He offered me his hand, and I took it in both of mine, yep, the way you hold onto a friend's hand—someone you know is a good man. His hand was big and fine, but even stronger than the both of mine put together. He smiled again in that special way he had: you could hardly see his teeth under that thick, trimmed mustache of his... He had a full, hearty laugh, like a true Mexican!

"I was so ashamed, and I asked him to forgive me for making him wait in the hot sun, because when they told me the President was outside, well, I thought it was just the town president from Puente d'Istla who had come for Monday's money for the plaza.

"The man kept smiling, and then, right away, to the heart of the matter.

"'Mister Delegate,' he said, all respectful, 'the engineers will be coming to Xoxocotla to put up the school, to make the plaza, and to put water in the pipes... The teacher or instructor will be here soon.'

"I nearly fell over backwards, to tell you the truth.

"When he left, the whole town followed him. Nobody was talking, and he went on ahead, with a good, firm step. Runnin' along, we could barely keep up with him. When he got into his Ford, he waved at us and drove off.

"When we went back, all the youngsters was laughing at us old ones 'cause we hadn't believed him. From that moment on I believed the young ones more, and now I pay attention to everything they say... T'other day one of them asked me: 'If a candidate came to Xoxocotla again, what would you ask him for, Uncle Luterio?'

"'Well, if you really want to know, I'd ask him to put up a statue, right there, where the lonesome little acacia tree used to be, of the President who came that time... A statue so we could all look at it, so it could be admired by all the children who come out of school, and so the pretty girls of Xoxocotla could cut every single one of the flowers on his saint's day, and lay them at his feet...'

"'That's a real nice thought, Uncle Luterio,' the boy answered; 'me and a lot of others know about reading because of him, and you and all the old ones have started to believe in men again, the way people used to believe in Emiliano, that one what come from Anenecuilco...' Can you believe it! Just look at how smart kids are today...!"

Don Eleuterio stood there silently for a few moments, lost in memories perhaps, then coming back to reality, he looked steadily at me and said:

"But let's see, friend. Can you find even one defect in the Xoxocotla plaza?"

"The only thing missing is a monument…"

"That's it, a monument!" he said as if he had made a discovery. "A monument… but on top of it, well, the statue of you know who… Then the Xoxocotla plaza would be the most beautiful in all of Morelos… Or what do you think, teacher?"

# The Sad Story of Pascola Cenobio ⤳

Cenobio Tánori lived in Bataconcica. Young and handsome, esteemed by men and a friend to women, the Yaqui liked to dazzle everyone at fairs, festivities and wakes, where he displayed his talent for dancing. It was reported that not a soul in the entire territory was his equal in the art of dancing, in performing the rugged, challenging ancestral dances… Tánori felt no greater glory than when he showed off his brilliance in the graceful leaps of the *pascola*, like a young, wild animal, shaking his legs lined with vibrant *ténavaris*, those small bells made from caterpillars or cocoons. Everyone admired the grace and elegance of Cenobio Tánori, his face covered by a horrifying goat-mask, as he raked his bare toes across the strip of loose dirt, recently sprayed with water, and sometimes covered with rose petals or wild shrubbery, to the music and rhythm of the pentaphonic reed-flute. And in the way his naked, Herculean torso undulated, shuddered, imitating the animal that has been brought back to life at its most passionate moments: anger, fear, heat, while the disk-timbrel on the dancer's left side resounded to the hard beat of the drum, the main musical instrument that accompanied totemic choreography.

Art has not been generous to those who practice it. The performances of Tánori generally received very little recompense: a steaming, mouthwatering pot of *guacavaqui*, a piece of roast beef cooked over hot coals, a couple of soft, warm flour tortillas, and a handful of cigarettes made with dark, pungent tobacco… That, along with the smiles and lowered eyes, the winks of women trying to attract the attention of that wild bohemian, that rustic, arrogant aesthete.

From village to village, from fair to fair went Cenobio Tánori, bringing his gaiety with him. He could tap his way through a *pascola* just as easily as he could perform the drawn-out, lively dances of *The Deer* or *The Coyote*, both primitive in origin, barbaric and sublime as the surroundings, as the blue-green environs, as the aggressive, beautiful vegetation around the little plaza in the squalid hamlet where the celebration took place: Babójori or Tórim, Corasape or El Baburo…

But one day—it was written in the stars—the vagabond's life sent out roots… It was in his own village, in Bataconcica, where the thought, where the will, of the world-traveler became bound—like a patch of cotton among the needles of a cactus—to the curled, full eyelashes over a pair of large, dark brown eyes, playful and restless, the eyes of Emilia Buitimea, that small, gentle girl who was able to catch what all the young, desirable Yaqui ladies wanted: Cenobio Tánori, the handsome, proud *pascola*.

Soon their names were linked in conversation: Emilia and Cenobio. "A good match," the old men remarked… But the old women, their feet planted firmly on the ground, hazarded a more realistic observation: "It's a pity Cenobio doesn't have much in the way of money… If it rains, what can he cover himself with?" Or else, the optimistic prediction: "The father-in-law, Benito Buitimea, he's rich and he'll be able to help the boy."

But Cenobio Tánori remained proud and fancy-free in spite of being in love; he would never consent to living off the father-in-law… He would never be a sponger in the house of his future wife.

It takes a lot to hold to these decisions; anyone who doesn't think so should ask Cenobio Tánori, the dancer who stopped going to fairs and carousing, who set out in search of what was needed for a wedding that, if not magnificent, would at least be worthy of Emilia Buitimea's class.

Spirited and determined, we see Tánori hanging up his beloved *ténavaris* forever, in order to hire himself out as a peon; working behind the yoke that he pushes as he labors to break through the big, deep land of the Yaqui Valley; carrying sacks stuffed full of garbanzos on his back, or gathering spikes of wheat into bundles... In general, people were astonished to see the eternal world-traveler submit to a drudgery that no one thought he would one day have to accept...

But the backbreaking work of a peon who plows does not bring much money... and the days passed by, to the boy's anxiety and to Emilia's silent sadness...

One day he thought his troubles had ended; it was when an outsider asked him to be his guide on an expedition through the mountain of El Mazocoba. He was trying to uncover veins of precious metals. The salary he offered was much greater than Cenobio Tánori's earnings from his hard farm labors, but there was one difficulty to his accepting it: the Indians, the *yoremes*, his own people, did not think highly of greedy white men digging in the ground of the sacred mountains, and even less acceptable to them was the idea that a Yaqui of Cenobio Tánori's distinction should lead the hated *yoris* down the hidden pathways and mysterious trails of El Mazocoba.

These circumstances kept Tánori from hiring himself out immediately when the opportunity arose... But necessity, the urgency hiding in the Indian's heart, encouraged by the miner's insistence and by the willingness of Emilia Buitimea, finally won out.

When he returned to Bataconcica, his purse was full. Three months of faithful service to the *yori* had not only brought him enough money for the wedding, but had also given him something to cope with the first expenditures in his future life at the side of Emilia... But in exchange for all this bounty, Cenobio Tánori had to face a very disagreeable situation: the old *yoremes*, those holders of an ever aggressive tradition, always on the defensive against the white man, received him coldly. Some even refused him the traditional gesture of welcome. The boy suffered these signs of scorn with stoicism. He was counting not only on the tenderness of his future wife, but also on the sympathy of the young people, a sympathy that reached great proportions when it came to the young women, those who were little affected by the stain that the old ones saw on the dancer's personality, or on his wedding bond with Emilia, for the first did not grieve them, and the second did not take the gilding from them...

And one afternoon, when Cenobio Tánori was waiting, in the middle of Calle Real in Bataconcica, for the chance to meet Emilia, he noticed the presence of Miguel Tojíncola, an enormous, old man with a black face carved up by a little axe who, staggering drunk, came right up to the dancer to poke fun at him with derisive laughter: "Here you see before you, ladies and gentlemen, the *yoreme* who made himself into a donkey, who made an ass of himself so the *yoris* could whip his butt and climb up on his back..." And another belly laugh thundered through the air, another cutting, stupid horse laugh, echoed by a hundred more from the mouths of the people who crowded together at the shouts of old Tojíncola.

Cenobio Tánori, looking a bit pale, eyes down, held back his emotions, because among the Yaquis, respect for one's elders reached religious proportions. But the drunk, paying no attention to his humble demeanor, continued implacably:

"So young and so strong, lending himself to the *yoris* like a little, old woman..."

Cenobio Tánori bit his lips and pretended not to hear the unrelenting crowd. Surrounding him were several children and some women who pointed their fingers at the hesitant boy, while they laughed gleefully at the mockery and ridicule spilling from the old man's toothless mouth:

"The water you drink will taste bitter; the *tortillas* will stick in your throat; you won't grow anything but crows on your little piece of ground, because the devil will piss everywhere you put your hand..."

The boy's submissiveness caused Tojíncola to become more and more animated all the time; disgusted at not being able to provoke a more assertive reaction from his victim, his lips—crimped with rage— opened with the greatest insult anyone could give in the Cahita tongue:

"*Torocoyori*," he said slowly. "*Torocoyori*," he repeated, which is to say: traitor, villain, sold out to the white man... "*Torocoyori...*

*Torocoyori...*" The insult, shouted repeatedly, was accompanied by a gob of spit that grazed the nearly beardless cheek of Cenobio Tánori...

Of course, the last recourses employed by Tojíncola were assertive enough to change his patient attitude. The boy crouched down, he took two steps back and sprang like a viper on the attack... No one could restrain him because the instinct that his willpower and good upbringing had held in check for long, anguishing moments, now rose to the surface...

The knife blade sank into the old man's chest, and he rolled in the dirt, red froth spilling from his mouth.

Cenobio Tánori did not attempt to flee. With the weapon in his right hand, he waited for the Indian authorities to apprehend him. Submissive, silent, but proud and dauntless, he followed the two constables who appeared at the scene where the incident had taken place... From a corner Emilia Buitimea, her eyes overflowing with tears, watched her fiancé. He raised his hand in a timid gesture of farewell... and marched behind his guards down Calle Real until they reached the prison. As the group following the *pascola* and his guards passed by, the old *yoreme* men were silent, the women spoke softly... And the young girls, the dancer's admirers, permitted their breasts to become inflamed with a sigh.

People came to the jail hole, where Indian justice had confined Cenobio Tánori, to show their affection for the disgraced *pascola*. The most frequent visitors were young women, girls who, timidly and somewhat fearfully, came to the jail with a bunch of wildflowers in their dark, little hands, a piece of fruit in season or a handful of cigarettes that they placed on the transom of the thick, wooden door, the barrier of the gloomy stall where the dancer awaited the day when the village would pronounce judgement on him... Cenobio Tánori, magnificent, proud as an offended god, silently and gravely accepted this tribute from his priestesses.

Of course, no one in Bataconcica talked about anything but the death of old Tojíncola and the future of his killer. The law of the Indians was final: since Cenobio Tánori had killed, he must be shot to death by a squad of soldiers... So said tradition, and so it must be carried out, unless the relatives of the deceased Miguel Tojíncola should grant mercy to the killer, and change his death penalty to a less cruel punishment... But there was not much hope that the prisoner would receive the clemency many wished for.

The dead man's family was made up of a widow and nine children whose ages ranged from sixteen down to two years old. The widow was an ugly woman of about fifty, with a huge body, large bones in every line, black in color, with the profile of an old eagle. Her brusque manner and always biting, tyrannical attitude left no one with any illusions about the chance that she might be forgiving. To the contrary, it was said that Marciala Morales, stubborn, strong-willed and vengeful, had promised to be merciless with the killer of her husband, Miguel Tojíncola.

Such a troubling future for the *pascola* brought cruel thoughts to the old men, bitter comments from the women, and tears, streaming tears from all the young ladies who, in spite of the matrimonial agreement between Cenobio Tánori and Emilia Buitimea, did not consider the man who had awakened sweet desire in them to be lost forever; the anxiety, for example, thathe craw of the blackbird, or in the wing of the butterfly...

In the meantime everything was made ready for the induction coucilmenwho would judge the homicide.

Yaqui justice is contained by a ring of rigid formulas and intransigencies. The village, assisted by the high authorities of the tribe, has the final word after discussions, after speeches that go on hour after hour, in a current of dramatic rigidity and then concession...

All right then, here we are in the tiny plaza of Bataconcica; a small crowd is pressing forward, waiting for the prisoner. In a place apart, we see the *cobanahuacs* or governors, serious and silent, and the severe village representatives who carry the entire civil power of the tribe on their shoulders. Representatives of the eight groups that make up the Yaqui nation are there: Bácum, Belem, Cócorit, Guíviris, Pótam,Ráhum, Tórim and Vícam... Near this impressive group is Marciala Morales, the widow, surrounded like a hen by her nine children; the oldest carry the smallest ones in their arms, crying and fussing. Nothing favorable for the fate of the dancer can be expected from her, from the widow of Miguel Tojíncola. This is evident from her cruel expression, from her defiant stance toward her clan, which humbles itself with a religious submission that the ugly woman, the nearly ancient woman, receives with a repugnant, hard and demanding demeanor.

At the front of the crowd we see a platoon of young soldiers, armed with Mausers, waiting sternly, in military fashion, for the sentence to be pronounced so that they may carry it out strictly, fatally.

A shadowy veil has fallen over the normally inscrutable faces of the Indians. This mark of uneasiness is especially noticeable in the young women, in those admirers of the ill-fated *pascola's* figure and grace... Emilia, the beloved and betrothed of Cenobio Tánori, is absent because the law forbids her to be here. Nevertheless, her father, old Benito Buitimea, rich and celebrated, does not hide his emotion before this dramatic event whose protagonist is the person that once wanted to be his son-in-law.

The funereal rattle of the small drum, the obligatory instrument in all transcendental acts of the Yaqui people, hushes the noise and the voices... Cenobio Tánori, alone, without guards, his head held high, letting the air play through his thick hair that hangs down until it brushes his shoulders, crosses the barrier where the people have opened a pathway for him. He is wearing the attractive finery in which he, time and again, has drawn the applause of the *yoremes*, the sinful thoughts of married women, the stifled, shamed sighs of unmarried women, and the admiration of the entire village. His shoulders and chest are naked, allowing his muscles to be seen clearly as they reveal themselves under the sheen of lightly perspiring skin. Around his neck hang necklaces of rattlesnake castanets. Between his legs, bowed, a cloth of fine wool held up by a strong rawhide belt, from which deer hooves and tails hang, and on the calves of his trousers, the *ténavaris* that, with the dancer's every step, jingle like tiny bells...

The dancer walks haughtily, with a firm, lithe step, to the center of the little plaza, to face his judge which will be the entire village...

No one is unaware, Cenobio Tánori included, that in spite of all the mitigating circumstances of the fatal actions, and notwithstanding, in addition, the admiration, the popularity, the sympathy that the *pascola* has with his people, no one can bend the legal precepts, no one can commute the death-sentence that is being prepared, except

Marciala Morales, the spiteful and horrible widow of Miguel Tojíncola, from whom nothing is to be expected, given her aggressive behavior...

Under these circumstances, one could hear the voice—dry from age and vibrant with emotion—of the Elder whom the law charges to make an accusation, to make an accusation that is always in defense of the interests, the peace and harmony of the group. After stating the facts as duly sustained by declarations and testimonies, he concluded by inciting them all:

"The laws that our fathers passed down to us as our most venerable heritage, say that the *yoreme* who kills a *yoreme* must die at the hands of the *yoremes*... But I, the Elder of Vícam, the Holy Land, I ask my people if they agree that brother Cenobio Tánori is to be killed just as brother Miguel Tojíncola died at his hands..."

The last words hung in the air for a few brief seconds; then they were followed by a noise like the swelling sea, and the distinct voice that proclaimed solemnly and decisively:

"Yes, Mauser..."

"Ehui, Mauser... *ehui*, Mauser... Mauser... Mauser..."

The clamor swept through the crowd. It fell on the bare head of Cenobio Tánori like a storm.

The Elder raised his hand, prematurely ageing and dry like the root of a *pitahayo*-plant, ready to let it fall as the final affirmation of the judgement of his people...

But then the young women, overcoming their shyness and timidity, begged in weak, trembling voices:

"Look at him, Marciala Morales, and then you will forgive him... All the women in the world will be grateful to you for your mercy... Save him from death because he's noble and brave... Look at him, Marciala Morales, he's as beautiful as a brightly colored bird and as graceful as a young deer."

The widow looked evilly at the group of women who were begging her. With clenched teeth, mute with fury, her gaze lost in a desert of hatred, she turned toward Cenobio Tánori who stood straight, proud, magnificent in the center of the little plaza...

That grimace on the old woman's face did not last long, because her wrinkled countenance was softened by an unexpected impulse. Her eyes, filled with unsuspected emotion, took on a disconcerting, human sheen. Her mouth lost its creases of acrimony and gave way to a foolish, lax, moronic expression...

The men, for their part, held to their terrible determination: "Mauser... *Ehui*, Mauser, Mauser... *ehui*, Mauser, Mauser..."

With the deafening noise, the Elder did not reach the point of bringing his hand down as a signal that the sentence had been carried out. There was a moment when no one would have been able to make out even one syllable from that roaring of beasts, that chattering of birds, that noise of flooding waters.

Suddenly a strident, grating voice filled the ears of the crowd. It was Marciala Morales who, on her feet and surrounded by her brood, but without moving her eyes that remained fixed on the dancer, was waving her arms, trying to silence the crowd...

All eyes turned toward her. She was magnificently ugly and barbaric:

"No," she shouted, "no Mauser... This man has left all these children of mine without a father. The law of our grandfathers also says that when a *yoreme* killed by another yoreme leaves behind a family, the killer must take care of the relatives of the dead man and marry his widow... I ask the people that Cenobio Tánori, the *pascola*, marry me, and that he protect me and the children of the deceased... No, no Mauser... Cenobio Tánori must take the place on my bench that old Miguel Tojíncola left... That is what I ask, and that is what they must give me."

There were a few seconds of absolute silence... and then mouths fell open, there was shouting, loud outbursts of laughter, catcalls, wisecracks, and then it all turned into a tumult of pandemonium. Cenobio Tánori tried to speak, but the clamor kept anyone from being able to hear his words.

The Elder let his hand drop wearily. He had carried out justice in strict accord with the ancestral code... Once again the noble Yaquis had held steadfast to their traditions.

The unneeded platoon paraded out to the roll of the drum. The people began to disperse.

Marciala Morales, followed by her large brood, went up to Cenobio Tánori and took him by the arm:

"Come on, you good boy," she said to him, "from now on you'll sleep next to me, so that you can rest from all the work you'll have to do to support this drove of kids you've inherited from old Tojíncola—may God keep him in His glory for all time to come..."

It was then that the celebrated *pascola* broke down. Head bowed, dragging his feet, ridiculous as a puppet, he followed his horrible executioner who smiled triumphantly while passing the young girls who would not look directly at a fallen star, at the death of an idol, shattered in the muscular, black hands of Marciala Morales...

The sky, a furious blue, covered the scene of the melodrama, and the sun burned down on the clumpy dirt in the little plaza.

# GLOSSARY

**Áxcale:** "Ahora está bien: así es." (It's all right now: that is how it is.)

**ayate:** Thin cloth made of agave fiber, woven by the Indians and used as bags for carrying fruit, etc.

**Cahita:** Indigenous tribe or group from Sonora, composed of Yaquis and Maya.

**Calles:** Plutarco Elías Calles. Mexican general and politician. President of the Republic from 1924 to 1928. His government was hostile to the Church.

**Epiphany:** January 6. The commemoration of Jesus revealing himself as the Christ-child to the Magi at Bethlehem. Also called "Twelfth Night." In Mexico, as in all Latin America, it is a more important celebration than Christmas.

**Esquipulas:** Town in Guatemala (Chiquimula).

**ixtle:** Fiber from the agave.

**Lacandón:** Mayan tribe.

**mecapal:** (Mex.) A sort of leather band with two cords attached, used by porters to carry a load more conveniently.

**metate:** A curved stone used for grinding maize for tortillas.

**nauyaca:** Extremely poisonous snake; appears to have four nasal passages (nahui, cuatro; yacatl, narices).

**nixtamal:** Corn partially cooked in lime water, from which tortillas are made.

**pascola:** A dance peculiar to the Sinaloa Indians and the Yaquis of Sonora, performed to the monotonous sound of drums and violins. The dancers carry small bells on their ankles, dress in extravagant costumes, and wear grotesque animal masks.

**pirul:** In Mexico, a tree imported from Peru.

**pitahayo:** Plant that produces a tropical fruit.

**Prencipal:** Principal: The person who is of greatest importance in a village, enterprise, etc.

**quina:** Jesuit's bark or Peruvian bark.

**sarahuato:** A large, hairy monkey.

**tata:** Father, Papa.

**tona:** Among the Indians of Guerrero and Oaxaca, an animal that in their superstitious rituals represents a sort of guardian angel.

**tostón:** In South America a *real de a cuatro*, or four silver reals, four bits; i.e. half a dollar or half an ounce.